Henry Foust

John Striven

Thomas Walton (+ Sir Richard)

The Tragickall History
of
Henry Fowst

Also by Griselda Heppel

Ante's Inferno

GRISELDA HEPPEL

The Tragickall History
of
Henry Fowst

Wood engraving for cover by Hilary Paynter

Cover design by Pete Lawrence

Matador
9 Priory Business Park,
Wistow Road, Kibworth Beauchamp,
Leicestershire. LE8 0RX
Tel: (+44) 116 279 2299
Email: books@troubador.co.uk
Web: www.troubador.co.uk/matador

Wood engraving for cover by Hilary Paynter
Cover design by Pete Lawrence

ISBN 978 1784623 043 (SB)
978 1784623 050 (HB)

British Library Cataloguing in Publication Data.
A catalogue record for this book is available from the British Library.

Printed and bound in the UK by TJ International, Padstow, Cornwall
Typeset in 12pt Aldine401 BT Roman by Troubador Publishing Ltd, Leicester, UK

Matador is an imprint of Troubador Publishing Ltd

For Nigel

Why, this is hell, nor am I out of it.
Marlowe, *The Tragical History of Doctor Faustus*

—

The Tragickall History of Henry Fowst

I

Why did I do it?

The years have passed and still I do not know. The sudden summons, the dart of joy, the sheer deliciousness of slipping into human shape once more, even for a short time – was that it?

When I saw who – or rather, what – had summoned me, and why... Well, it was a shock, to say the least. That might account for it. I expected the man – now grown wiser and willing to consider my proposal – and what did I find? A boy. A mere boy. What did he want with infinite knowledge, infinite power? That I, of all spirits, should be at the beck and call of a child no more than twelve years old!

Ah. I remember now. Snaring the souls of men and women – not much challenge there. Most are hell-bound long before they call for me. But an innocent – now there's a prize. An investment worth any number of grown men. How could I guess he would turn out such a fool, leaving me a job half done?

Yet all is not lost. The matter can wait. Down here time has no meaning. Forty years or four hundred or four thousand, it is the same. All that counts is the call when it comes.

I can wait.

by Griselda Heppel

1

How It All Began

Walton Hall, December 1585

John Striven leaned over the half door, its wooden edge digging into his ribs. His eyes, adjusting to the dim light, picked out the horse's outline, the white diamond on its brow, the gleam in its dark pupil as the long, arched neck curved round.

'Over here,' he whispered. 'That's it.' A gentle clopping over wood and straw and a soft, velvety nose nudged the palm of his hand. 'Sorry, my beauty, I've nothing for you. Only this.' Reaching up, John patted the smooth black neck. He was so close now he could feel the horse's breath on his cheek, its warmth mingling with the smell of sweet hay that could never mask the sour odour of dung in any stables, however grand they might be – and grand these certainly were.

Giving a last pat, he stood back and looked about him. Eight loose boxes at this end alone, perhaps the same at the other, beyond the central passage, each with its own window in which the Walton coat of arms stood out in red and blue panels amidst the clear glass. From the contented snorts and munching sounds drifting from the far end, his and his father's horses were being given a good rub-down and a mouthful of hay by Sir Richard's stable lads.

John felt his lips twist into a smile. If all went well today, Bramble and Molly might soon feel quite at home in these fine surroundings. His father had been gone – what, fifteen, twenty minutes? He must be with Sir Richard now, perhaps in that great library whose books mounted so high a special gallery had to be built to reach them; a thing unheard of anywhere before.

Turning, he leaned back against the stall, the horse's warm breath tickling his cheek. From here he could see through the wide stable door into the yard, past the brew house on the right, to the great hexagonal tower at the corner of the west wing of Walton Hall, rising into the cold January sky. Behind it the domed roof of a matching tower glinted in the sun, while closer to, the main block ran at right-angles between west and east wing, its roof sprouting smaller turrets interspersed with high chimneys.

So many tall, mullioned windows, so many rooms; now he understood the rumours among the household at Combe of a library larger than any chamber there! What books might it contain? The Roman and Greek authors, certainly; books of devotion such as, according to his father, a gentleman should possess. But – and here John felt a familiar stirring inside, an excitement he

4

couldn't explain – people at Combe had whispered of other subjects dear to the master's heart: strange, magical works on mathematics and natural philosophy and the movement of the stars…

Crash. On the far side of the yard a gate banged open. Chickens squawked and ran in all directions as a boy came charging towards him, glossy, shoulder-length black hair flying under his cap, the ends catching on his stiff white ruff. About his own age, John guessed, but much more richly dressed in his blue velvet doublet and hose. Under brows drawn together the boy's dark eyes were fixed on the stable entrance, as if searching for someone. His mouth was a thin, tight line.

John's heartbeat quickened. He shouldn't be here. Sir Richard didn't expect him, and his father, yielding to his pleas to be taken along, had warned him to keep out of the way. Yet news would have reached the house that not one, but two people had arrived at the stables. Was he about to be hauled into the master's presence for reproof? To bring shame upon his father?

Slipping to the empty stall opposite, he flattened himself against the panels. Out of sight of the doorway now he might escape notice. He held his breath.

Footsteps skidded to a halt on the threshold. 'Walt!'

John jumped. The boy must be a good ten feet away, round the side of the stall, but it felt as if he'd screeched into John's ear.

'M-master Thomas!' With a hasty click of the half door a stable lad emerged from Bramble's stall on the other side of the passage and came striding over. 'I did not—'

'No, you didn't, did you?' The boy launched himself at the stable lad, fists directed at his midriff. 'Flash has had her puppies and you never sent me word! You were to tell me at once, not leave Abel to bring the news!'

The stable lad doubled up in pain. John's jaw tightened. Walt might be taller and sturdier but his assailant certainly knew where to punch.

Walt gasped. 'Master Thomas, I – pray you, it – happened but two hours since. 'Tis best – they are not disturb—' he broke off in a yelp at a well-aimed kick to his shin.

'Out of my way!' Giving a final shove, the boy headed down the passage past the feed bins. 'Flash! *Flash!* Where are you? Ah!'

At the end of the passage a door lay ajar. John caught a glimpse of saddles racked along the wall of the room beyond, the gleam of stirrups and bridles, before the boy hurled himself through, letting the door bang behind him. A cry of delight – followed by a sound that pierced John's heart. A whimpering, pleading, animal sound.

In eight strides he reached the door and pushed it open.

On a piece of sacking in the corner of the tack room lay a spaniel, pale golden belly turned out to suckle the small, mewing things that blindly sought her swollen dugs. Her copper head, which should have been resting on her paws, or nuzzling her newborn, instead stretched upwards, moving to and fro. A low growling came from her exhausted throat, all the resistance she could offer to the figure kneeling beside her, one hand rummaging among the puppies, the other flicking her muzzle with a shape that was long and thin.

A whip.

Darkness flooded John's vision. He was aware of nothing, not the sound of his boots stamping across the floor, nor the constriction in his lungs; only the face that swung round at him, its fine features distorted in a cry of rage, as John seized the whip and flung it away.

The boy leapt to his feet. 'By heaven! Who are you? Hobbs! *Hobbs!* An intruder!'

John took a step back. His chest rose and fell so hard it felt as if his ribs might burst. 'I'm no intruder,' he panted. 'My name is John Striven. My father is bailiff of Sir Richard Walton's manor at Combe. The master bid us – bid my father' – he corrected himself, colouring – 'here, since he is in need of a steward and thinks my father—'

He stopped. He was wasting what little breath he could spare as Thomas gazed beyond him, expecting Hobbs to answer his summons. Which was unlikely, since no sooner had the head groom welcomed John and his father than he'd been summoned to the hall for the servants' dinner.

Thomas glared at him. 'I don't care who you are,' he spat, 'you have no right to interfere with my sport.'

'*Sport*?' John couldn't contain himself. 'You call it sport to treat a poor animal like that?'

Thomas turned a deathly white. Under his right eye a muscle twitched. 'How – *dare* – you' – the words scraped his throat as if they choked him. He reached down to the floor.

John didn't see it coming. A crack and a line of pain across his left cheek. Clapping a hand to his face, he felt his fingers slide on blood. He gasped as Thomas prepared to strike again with the riding crop that he – fool! – hadn't cast far enough away, and didn't wait. He ran from the room, down the passage and into the yard.

Footsteps thudded behind him. 'Come back, you knave, I'm not finished yet!'

There. Straight ahead, a gate in the wall, the one by which Thomas had stormed into the yard. John raced towards it, scattering chickens, startling a solitary stable lad sweeping the cobbles, and flung it open. Too late he saw his mistake. The house surrounded him on all three sides, casting a deep shadow over bare, triangular herb beds between which a path led up to the door.

No help for it. The herb garden blurred into a grey-brown mass as John tore up the path, skidding on ice patches, the stone columns framing the entrance jigging up and down before him. Up the steps, through the door and into the dark-panelled corridor – but where then? From the right came a murmuring, the clink of trenchers and tankards, a savoury aroma – of course, that way must lie the hall where the household was eating dinner, and at the end of the corridor, the kitchen. They'd think him some vagabond if he came flying in among them mud-spattered, hat awry, cheek smeared with blood!

Through the herb garden rang his pursuer's voice. 'Base, cowardly wretch, flee and blab to the kitchen maids! Clinging to their skirts won't save you!'

John looked left. Here the corridor stretched into gloom, only partly relieved by pale light filtering through lattice panes, and he hurried down it, flinching at the tap of his boots on the floor. Surely somewhere along here he could hide... Ah! On the right, a recess, two steps up and a heavy oak door. Seizing the iron ring, he turned it, slipped through and, closing the door, leaned back, lungs pumping, ears straining for the sound of running feet outside.

Nothing. He waited, hardly daring to breathe. All was still. *Yes.* It would take his pursuer some time to hunt him through the kitchen and the service rooms around it. Perhaps he might even lose interest and return to his cruel game in the tack room. Pray Hobbs might be on hand then to give that poor bitch some protection.

Letting his fingers uncurl from where they pressed against the wood John opened his eyes.

And blinked.

CHAPTER TWO

The Christmas Present

Northwell School, about 420 years later

Well, better get it over with.

Henry Fowst hoisted his school bag more comfortably across his shoulder and walked through the gate. Keeping his eyes on the ground, he made straight for the tunnel between the dining room and music blocks, reaching the playground before any of the people streaming in on either side of him noticed. So far so good.

Looking up, he was briefly dazzled. Away to the left, beyond the river, the rising sun broke through the clouds, sending a beam that caught the tip of the turret just above him. Screwing up his eyes, he let his gaze linger, feeling his spirits lift at the sheer incongruity of the sight. How many other schools could boast a turret on their roof? Or a pair of tall, spiral-patterned chimneys, looking totally out of place with the rest of the main building, let alone the glass and concrete classroom block?

He gave a wry smile. Funny how more than a year

after winning a scholarship into this whole new world of traditions, uniforms, old-fashioned games of marbles and conkers, acres of grass and meadows rolling down to the river, the overall magic of the place could still take him by surprise. Especially when the atmosphere in some parts – the library, for instance – went, well, beyond magical. Spooky, even.

Enough. He should get a move on. Between him and the classrooms people clustered together, comparing their new gadgets, tablets – whatever. The trick was to make it past without any of them looking up.

'Hey, Hamf – I mean, Henry – what's the hurry?'

Thanks Charlie, thought Henry, *for remembering to use my real name. Eventually.* 'Nothing,' he said out loud. 'It's cold, that's all.' He shivered, a bit too obviously.

Not that Charlie noticed. 'Uh-huh.' His light brown eyes flicked back to the notice board at the mouth of the tunnel. If he bent any closer, he'd bash his nose on the glass.

'Charlie, you *know* you'll be in the football team,' said Henry. 'Give Ralph a chance to put the lists up.'

'What, is he here?' Charlie looked round.

Henry groaned. 'Don't know, I haven't seen him. But the team's hardly going to be fixed on the first day of term, is it?'

'Do I hear my name?' A tall, fair-haired figure emerged from the tunnel opening. Shirtsleeves rolled up in spite of the cold, he held his anorak across his shoulder with one hand while the other was plunged

11

into his trouser pocket. 'Hi, guys,' he smiled. 'How was Christmas?'

'Hi Ralph!' said Charlie. 'Great, thanks.'

'Yeah,' mumbled Henry. 'Charlie was just wondering—'

'Who said I was?' Charlie cut in. 'You were won-dering, more like—'

'*Me*?' cried Henry. 'No, I—'

'Whoa, slow down, guys,' Ralph put up his hand. 'Wait for the trials, eh?' With a wink at Charlie he strolled off towards the classroom block.

Henry gazed after Ralph's retreating figure. 'Well you're in,' he said. 'That's obvious.'

'You might make it too,' said Charlie. 'You never know.'

'Yeah, right. A marbles team, maybe.' Henry's hand went to the bag in his pocket, freshly replenished from Christmas Day with an emperor, three galaxies, a bloody Mary and a few others. Rachel must have saved her pocket money for weeks.

'Oh yeah, let's have a quick game.' Charlie nodded over Henry's shoulder. 'Look, no one else is. What've you got?'

Turning, Henry hesitated. Between the sandpit on the far side of the music block and the edge of the games field lay a tempting stretch of tarmac, empty and shining in the early morning light. A few juniors had dropped their school bags to mess around in the sand – cover for him and Charlie, if they needed it. But the crowd flowed in the opposite direction towards the classrooms and no one gave that part of the playground a glance.

Charlie got there first. Rummaging in his small

drawstring bag he drew out a giant cat's eye. It flashed in the sun as he rolled it across the frozen ground to a distance about four metres away. 'Try *that*.'

Henry couldn't suppress a grin. There'd been a time when a marble that size would have taken his breath away. That Charlie should risk his best treasure at the start of a game! Now he knew better. He felt inside his own marble bag; ah, a comet. That would do.

At the sight of the medium-sized, translucent white sphere licked by tongues of red and blue Charlie gave a pitying smile. 'Come on, you've got better than that. It's half the size of mine.'

Henry crouched down, the marble between his thumb and forefinger. 'If you think' – he closed one eye – 'I'm going to risk any of the ones I got for Christmas' – he took aim – 'on your poxy, oversized cat's eye—'

'You have. Got to be. Kidding,' drawled a voice.

Henry's marble whizzed across the tarmac, missing Charlie's by a hair's breadth.

'And he can't even shoot straight.'

No mistaking that voice. No need to look up and see Jake standing there, mock-disbelief written all over his pasty face. Grabbing his marble bag, Henry jabbed it at his pocket. It refused to go in.

'Yeah, in your position I'd want to hide the evidence too. Hear that, Ralph? Hamface got *marbles* for Christmas.'

Henry froze. Not Ralph. The one person he'd been sure was safely out of the way and here he was, minus bag and anorak, walking back across the playground towards them. A familiar, hateful warmth rushed up Henry's neck to his cheeks, reminding him – as if he needed it, right now! – of that stupid nickname. Hand clamped to his pocket he waited for Ralph's amused – or worse, pitying – reaction.

But Ralph seemed not to have heard. He walked slowly, concentrating on something in his hand. A phone, by the look of it – but not just any phone. Its slim shape and smoothly rounded edges spoke of the latest in technology and design.

Charlie paused in the act of scooping up the two marbles left on the tarmac. 'You got *that* for Christmas? Wow, Ralph! I wish my dad owned a computer company.'

'Yeah,' said Ralph. 'It was either this or a laptop. Tough call, really.'

'Hamface got marbles,' Jake repeated, even louder this time. 'How sad is that?'

Not sad at all, actually, when your sister gave them to you because she's only seven years old. When it's the one present you get that isn't something you need, like new jeans or trainers. Jamming the bag into his pocket, Henry held his hand over it, fist clenched.

'C'mon Henry,' Charlie murmured, giving him back his comet, 'let's go in.'

'Yeah,' said Henry. His feet itched to break into a run. But that would be stupid.

Ralph shrugged. 'If that's what he asked for, why not?' He flashed Henry a smile before going back to flicking his fingers over his phone.

Henry grinned back. *Yeah, why not?* he thought. *In your FACE, Jake!* His step lightened as he crossed the playground.

'Sure,' sniggered Jake. 'I asked for marbles once. 'Bout five years ago. When I was *eight*.'

Charlie opened his eyes very wide. 'So it can count!' he called over his shoulder. 'Hey, Jake, can you spell whole words too?'

It took a few seconds for Jake's grin to fade and a red flush to spread across his cheek. He lunged forward. '*Shut it,* you—'

'Let's go,' said Charlie. Gripping Henry's sleeve, he steered him to the classroom block and through the door. 'Jake's rubbish at marbles. Gave up playing in Year Five. Reckon I've still got a few of his in my bag.'

'What I can't understand,' said Henry, 'is why a guy like Ralph puts up with a jerk like him.'

'Dunno. Out of pity, maybe?' Charlie snorted.

'Good morning, boys.'

Henry and Charlie pulled up short.

At the front of the classroom, navy blue cape draped over the back of her chair, sat Mrs James, the deputy head.

'Where's Mr Matthews?' said Charlie.

'Sit down boys. Thank you.'

Henry hung up his anorak. Collapsing on to his chair, he caught Charlie's eye. This didn't look good.

Mrs James began the register. Her crisp, bright tones grated on Henry's ears. It should be Mr Matthews sitting there, long legs bent under the desk like a stick insect, his few remaining hairs brushed across his head in wisps, his voice a vague murmur. Not this interloper who, after a full term at Northwell, still seemed incapable of pronouncing a single name correctly.

'Now,' said Mrs James, closing the book, 'I'm sorry to tell you that Mr Matthews slipped on the ice over the holidays and broke his leg, which gives me the chance to do some teaching for a change.' Under tortoiseshell glasses her smile swept the room. 'And as my class –'

Henry winced. Her class? *Hers*?

'– you can be the first to know the exciting news. I've persuaded the headmaster to revive the Northwell Prize, set up by Dr Northwell in 1920, for the best essay on the history of the school. The deadline is the Monday before half-term; the prize…' she paused, clearly savouring the moment. 'Twenty pounds.'

A sigh rippled round the room. It sounded like the deflating of a large gas balloon.

'I guess twenty quid was a lot of money in 1920,' said Ralph.

'Yeah, right,' scoffed Jake.

Something fluttered inside Henry. *Twenty pounds*. Peanuts to most people at Northwell but for him – hey, that was a mobile phone! A basic one, of course, and he'd have to save to top it up – but still a phone.

Not just that. In his mind's eye he saw his father, the deep-cut lines on his forehead smoothed away and a light in his grey eyes no one had seen for months. *Go for it, Henry. You know you can do it.*

16

The fixed smile left Mrs James's lips. 'It's not just the money, Jeff,' she snapped. 'I expect all of you to enter. Which is why your first history lesson will be taking place in the library.'

Silence. Charlie stopped swinging his legs under his chair. All eyes in the room focussed on the deputy head who beamed back, gratified at last to have gained everyone's attention.

A slim brown arm went up. 'Mrs James, did you say the – library?' asked Meena.

Mrs James frowned. 'Of course. Surely you've had lessons there before? Goodness me, don't look so worried,' she added as Meena slowly shook her head. 'It's only books. They don't bite, you know.' She let out a tinkle of laughter.

No one joined in. People looked at each other or down at their hands.

'What on earth is the matter with you all?' cried Mrs James. 'Anyone would think I'd asked you to join me in some frightful dungeon – ah. I see. Don't tell me you believe all that business about the library being haunted?' She tapped a pencil on the desk. 'Harry, what about you? Harry!'

Oh help, she means me. Forgetting he was sitting down, Henry leapt to attention, banging his knee on his desk. People tittered as he felt the telltale heat creep up his neck. 'Um, n-not haunted exactly,' he said. That strange feeling he got on those rare occasions he'd braved the fierce librarian, Mrs D'Arcy, and gone in for a look round, that sense of something – or someone – watching him: mightn't that be down to the gloomy atmosphere? Mrs D'Arcy's three-pupil rule didn't help; how could an empty library *not* feel, well, a bit spooky? Maybe if they all went in together the spookiness would melt away.

Clearly Mrs James thought so. 'Right,' she said, 'I've had quite enough of these silly rumours. I don't want to read twenty-six identical downloads from Wikipedia, I want to see some original research, using real books. You are lucky to have one of the best-preserved Elizabethan libraries in the country. And just because it's old – well, of course, it must be haunted. Utter nonsense.'

The bell went. Chairs scraped back.

'See you there, straight after assembly!' Tucking the register under her arm, Mrs James stalked out of the room.

Henry looked round. Never mind the library, what were his chances with the Northwell Prize? Obviously Jake wouldn't bother. And Ralph certainly didn't need the money. Charlie – er, no. His gaze fell on a pair of shining black plaits framing a perfectly oval face, eyes cast down in thought as their owner walked towards the door.

Meena. Yeah, she'd enter.

CHAPTER THREE

The Library

Walton Hall, December 1585

Never in his life had John seen so many books. Great, thick, heavy volumes, half as tall as he, their contents sealed with chains, lining the walls to head height and more; while above – there it was! A gallery bordered by oak railings and balustrade, running along the three walls around where he stood, reached by matching staircases that curved towards him from halfway down the room. A few steps up one of these and several rows of smaller books lay within easy grasp, glimpses of costly velvet and silk bindings standing out among the lines of grey vellum.

Did he dare? The master's library, the part of Walton Hall he'd longed above all to see! Tiptoeing over to the right-hand stairs, John paused. On the floor, in the curve of the staircase, stood an oak lectern holding a pale, oblong shape. Not a book as such. Rather, a collection of yellowing pieces of parchment folded together; an old deed, a map perhaps – in which case, what was it doing here? It belonged surely with other estate papers, in Sir Richard's study or accounting chamber.

Something about its very ordinariness held John's gaze. Slipping his hand between the folds, he opened it, releasing a cloud of dust. Untouched for some time then, years even. For a few seconds he stared at the creamy-grey surface while a tingling sensation ran up and down his body.

This was no ordinary document. Faded brown handwriting, yes, he'd expected that, but – the drawings. Not plans of the Walton Hall estate, showing house, fields, river, barns... Instead a strange mixture of images: the sun surrounded by flames, a crescent moon, a woman with long flowing hair; and, larger than all of these, a robed man holding a sword whose tip outlined a five-point star, held within a circle, on the ground before him. *"The menes by whiche the Naturall Philosopher may Summon an Angellick Spirit to assiste him in Grete Perplexitie"* lay scrawled alongside.

John pressed his hands either side of the lectern. This manuscript – could it be Sir Richard's work? His own handwriting, a record of methods he used here, at Walton Hall, to make the natural world yield up its secrets? If so, those magical rumours at Combe were well-founded!

And yet not. This was a library, not a school room. From the faded ink and discoloured parchment, the hand that had written this belonged to a man who lived a long time ago. Doubtless Sir Richard took a mere collector's interest in it, nothing more.

Folding the parchment back over, he made again for the stairs – and stopped. In the far end of the room a flash of metal caught his eye. Low winter sunlight shone through tall windows, sending diamond patterns across the floor, interspersed with the bright red and blue of the Walton arms; and on a long oak table stretching the width of the bay, unfamiliar shapes – round, angular, metallic – glinted against the polished surface.

John's heart leapt. This was better than any book! A collection of mathematical instruments, some he'd never seen before, lying within touching distance… In seconds he stood by the table, the globe's leathery surface warm under his palm. With a flick of the fingers, he smiled as the world spun at his touch, before letting his eye travel to another globe, the shadow of this one, a skeletal version even, made of a mass of metal bands. What could that signify? Or those two staffs lying next to it, joined at right angles to each other – some measuring tool, perhaps, like his father used to survey the land at Combe. Yet the sheet of brass, crammed with markings, spread out between the staffs – he couldn't make out its use at all. What might Sir Richard wish to measure in such close detail?

From his left came a soft click as of a door being quietly closed. He whirled round.

'Well, well. A visitor, I see.'

Framed against an entrance at this end of the room,

that John, in his eagerness, had failed to notice, stood Sir Richard, one arm thrown out to form a barrier. Behind this John's father, pale-faced, the muscles of his jaw tensed, seemed to be only just holding himself back – barrier or no – from seizing his son.

John felt the blood drain from his limbs. 'S-Sir – I ask your pardon, I –' What could he say? Had he set out on purpose to destroy everything for his father, he couldn't have done better than this – thrusting himself in here unbidden, mud-flecked, his clothes crumpled and disordered!

Sir Richard dropped his arm. 'Why didn't you tell me, Striven, your son was with you? Young John, isn't it?'

'Yes, sir.' John bowed his head.

'Left out in the cold this half-hour while your father and I've been comfortable in my study, poring over account books and estate papers and I know not what, to give him a good understanding of his new office. Eh, Striven?' He nodded over his shoulder. 'I don't wonder at your son's seeking shelter in here. Time well spent, what's more,' he added, with a glance at the table. 'As careful an examination of my instruments as I could make myself.'

John raised his head. Looking from Sir Richard to his father, he read in their expressions – one smiling, the other a mixture of astonishment and relief – that all was not lost. 'Sir,' he stammered, 'I – that is, thank you, sir.'

Stripes of sunlight fell across Sir Richard's doublet, turning the fawn to gold, as he walked to the table. 'Tell me then, young scholar, what is your – God's Truth, my boy, what have you done to your face?'

John raised his hand to his cheek. The blood had dried but the cut felt raw, swollen.

A line appeared between Sir Richard's bushy eyebrows as he studied the wound, and he pursed his lips as if the pain struck his own skin, not the twelve-year-old boy's standing before him.

'I –' John faltered. A voice rang in his brain, spiteful, mocking. *Flee and blab to the kitchen maids, cowardly wretch*! 'I – was running in the herb garden, sir,' he said. 'I slid on the ice and hit something sharp.' He squirmed inwardly. Could he do no better than that?

But the kind face before him cleared. 'Running in the –? Well, Striven, I'm glad to see your son is still a boy as well as a scholar,' Sir Richard chuckled. 'Come now, let's hear what you make of my instruments: this one for instance.' He held up the measuring tool. 'You handled it with some skill.'

'Is it a – a cross staff, sir?'

'Near the mark.' Sir Richard replaced the instrument. 'It is a quadrant. For measuring the angle of a star. That interests you, I see. In that case' – he reached further down the table – 'I have something else for you. An astrolabe.'

John opened his eyes wide. In the master's hands lay a brass disc, the size of a small platter, its rim divided into equal markings, its surface engraved with multiple curved lines that crossed over each other and fanned out, like a spider's web. Snugly inside the disc was fitted a kind of wheel with strange, flat hook shapes and points curling out from both rim and hub. It was beautiful.

'Sir,' his father found his voice at last. 'It's good of you to take such pains with my ill-mannered son but his conduct, for which' – he glared at John – 'he'll answer to me later, does not deserve it.'

John dropped his gaze. His shoulders tensed, preparing for the beating to come.

Sir Richard put a hand on his father's arm. 'No, don't punish him, Striven. He meant no harm. God knows it's rare for me to chance on another soul who takes delight in these things. See now' – he held the astrolabe towards him – 'take hold the rete and turn it.'

John's hand flew to the small knob projecting from the brass wheel. Turning it, he caught his breath.

'You see? Those spikes mark the positions of the brightest stars. They are now moving over the sky underneath them. You can plot how they move during the passage of a day and in relation to the sun—'

A crash came from beyond the wall directly opposite the master's study. John looked up just in time to see the double doors of yet a third way into the library fly open to reveal Thomas, framed in a vestibule, beyond which another set of doors showed a glimpse of the great hall. 'Father, there's—' Seeing John, he broke off, mouth open.

John's heart slammed in his chest. *Father*! Of course, this boy dressed in rich velvet, fine lace bordering his ruff and sleeves, behaving with such freedom to all around him, who else could he be but the master's son? Soon, soon the story of their heated encounter in the stables would be out and it would all be up for his own father. For how could Sir Richard countenance as steward one whose son dared to challenge his own in such a manner?

Sir Richard, who at the crash of the doors had all but dropped the astrolabe, briefly closed his eyes. 'Thomas,' he sighed, 'I've asked before that you enter with less – why, look at you!' His face creased into a smile. 'You make a pair with John here!'

Panting, hatless, his ruff limp and clothes awry, Thomas glanced at John and didn't reply.

Seeing the look, Sir Richard put down the astrolabe, threw back his head and laughed, the point of his tawny beard quivering. 'But this is splendid!' he cried. 'You two have met! What was it, hide and seek? Well, Tom, from the time it's taken you to track your quarry down I'd say he was a match for you!'

A pause. John felt Thomas's eyes on him.

'Perhaps,' said Thomas. 'Or perhaps he's just been fortunate.'

Sir Richard slapped his thigh. 'A match!' he cried. 'Why didn't I think of it before? Tom, you've been too much alone these last six years. A playfellow is just what you need. Since your dear mother's death, and the child too, that would have been your brother' – at this a quiver of impatience shot through Thomas's shoulders, unnoticed by Sir Richard who had turned to John's

25

father. 'What think you, Striven? Our sons are the same age, I believe. A new beginning all round, you and the rest of your family in the house apportioned you on the estate, your son here with us! Doctor Thorne can teach two as well as one, and young John will learn more than he ever could at the grammar school.'

John stood still. Playfellow to this – this savage! A boy who tormented animals and played chase with a riding crop!

And yet... His eye slid to the table where the instruments gleamed; from there to the shelves running along the far end of the room where row upon row of books stretched into the darkness. That all this could be his to discover! And other, deeper mysteries, ones he'd never come across before today: curious, ancient manuscripts, like the one lying on the lectern. A great wave rose inside him as he fixed his gaze on his father's profile, every nerve strained to hear the words that would decide his fate.

So that he barely noticed Sir Richard, frowning slightly, walk over to the lectern, take the manuscript and slip into the shadows beyond the staircase.

Returning, Sir Richard rubbed his hands together and beamed. 'Well, Striven?'

John's father stood, lips slightly parted, looking from Sir Richard to John and back again. His beard trembled as he struggled to frame the words. 'Sir,' he brought out at last, 'such kindness to my son is more than he—'

'Nonsense, Striven. My son needs company. And

yours has a thirst for knowledge you can't satisfy. See, by the light in his eye – by Jove, sir, if a little of your ardour could rub off on Tom while you learn together— '

'A-astronomy, sir? And – and mathematics?' The words rushed out, John couldn't hold them back. 'And the use of all your instruments?' Such learning was well worth a few cuts and bruises! And perhaps, once Thomas was used to his company…

'Not so fast!' Sir Richard chuckled. 'Subjects of the quadrivium come later, at university. If you *strive* as hard as your name suggests, eh, my boy' – the chuckle broadened into a laugh it was impossible not to return, and Sir Richard paused, mightily pleased with his joke – 'I see no reason why you shouldn't both enrol together, in due course. What say you, Thomas? Do you like the plan?'

John stiffened. He felt Thomas's gaze travel up and down his body as if seeing him for the first time, taking in the thick wool of his doublet and hose, the coarse linen ruff clinging to his neck, the colour rising to his cheeks until they must surely match the bright copper of his hair.

Thomas smiled. 'Yes, Father,' he said. 'If that is your wish.'

If… John's eyes met Thomas's. Something in their glitter sent a shiver down his spine.

CHAPTER FOUR

Lavinia D'Arcy Gets a Shock

'Trust her to be late,' said Charlie. 'Not that I'm dying to get in there.' Hands in his pockets, he leaned against the corridor wall and gazed out of the window on to the playground.

'Could be worth a look,' said Henry. 'All those old books.'

'For you maybe. Can't say they get me excited. Though it might be fun to get into the gallery.'

'Oh yes,' said Meena, 'the books they won't let us see!'

Charlie raised an eyebrow. 'Not scared then, Meena?'

'N-no.' Meena's cheeks went a little pink. 'A bit maybe. But if we're all together… and I'm sure it's just nonsense, like Mrs James said. Oh,' she rolled her eyes, 'where is she? It's not as if she's got far to come.'

No distance at all. Beyond the library, outside which the class had congregated, the corridor continued the length of the assembly hall, ending at the door leading into the lobby. Peering past the groups of boys and girls lounging against the wall, Henry saw the door swing open and the deputy head at last hurry through.

'Ah, here you are,' she said. ('Just as if it was *us* keeping *her* waiting,' Meena hissed.) 'All present? Good.' Mounting the two steps to the library door, she reached for the heavy iron ring of the handle.

There was a general intake of breath. 'Old Lavvy will go *mental*,' murmured Charlie. 'It's bad enough when just one of us tries to get in.'

'Mrs James,' said Meena, 'can we go anywhere in the library? Anywhere at all?'

'Absolutely, Mindy,' Mrs James pushed open the door. 'Books are there for everybody.'

Henry caught Charlie's eye. This could be interesting. Even so he felt his chest tighten as he followed Mrs James in, unable to stop himself glancing into the dark corners either side to see if – if what? There was nothing there. Only the rest of the class pouring in around him, giggling and scuffing their shoes on the wooden floor, dispelling any sense of gloom. He smiled, in spite of himself. Maybe all the place needed was a few people milling around.

From the expression on Lavinia D'Arcy's powder-pale face, this wasn't at all how she saw it. Her red mouth, normally fixed in a disagreeable line, dropped open, giving her the look of one of those giant painted faces in fairground booths, waiting for tennis balls to be lobbed at them. '*What – is the meaning – of this*?' she barked.

'Ah, Lavinia…' Mrs James glided forward, her tall shape taking up most of the librarian's view.

'Quick,' whispered Meena. 'We won't get much time.'

Henry, Meena and Charlie stood at the north end of the library, the sheer length of which made it seem narrower than it really was. Facing them, halfway down the room, two flights of stairs curved up to the left and right, leading to a book-lined gallery that ran back along the three walls around them. In the bay in the southern end, Mrs D'Arcy sat at an L-shaped desk, the straightness of her back echoed by the long mullioned windows that reached down to the floor behind her. Through the small, shimmering panes the light fell grey and cheerless; not even the red and blue stained glass insertions could make any difference. To the left of the desk, a door led into the headmaster's office, which Mr Robertson used every morning to cross the library and enter the hall through double doors on the right: an unusual design that must, Henry decided, have more to do with the age of the rooms than the importance of Mrs D'Arcy. Not that anyone dared tell her this.

Leaning on the librarian's desk, Mrs James waved behind her. 'My class, 8M. I've arranged to hold their lesson here so they can research the history of the school.'

'You've *what*?' Mrs D'Arcy swivelled from side to side as she attempted to keep track of the figures swarming among the book stacks.

'Henry, Charlie,' Meena whispered, nodding up at the gallery, 'what do you reckon?'

The right-hand staircase stood a couple of paces away.

At the top, just before the gallery began, it gave on to a recess cut deep into the wall – presumably to make even more space for books – matched by another recess opposite. Two pools of darkness, each one offering plenty of cover for all three of them. If they made it that far.

Henry hesitated. It wasn't just the darkness. Something about its very stillness held him back, a stillness untouched by the rustling and chattering that had chased the shadows from the rest of the library. It was as if an invisible shield, brittle as glass, surrounded the whole gallery, ready to shatter at their approach.

From the far end of the room two voices rose and intertwined like barbed wire.

'*Three pupils*, Mrs James! That is the maximum I allow at any one time and you *burst in* here with your *whole class*—'

'But Lavinia, this is a school library, a vital educational resource.'

'Perhaps.' Mrs D'Arcy's tone implied this was arguable. 'However, it also contains the Walton Collection, books dating back to the sixteenth century. Even their Victorian leather bindings haven't totally destroyed their value. You will understand, then, why I cannot have young people ranging freely all over the library and indeed there are some areas *completely forbidden* to pupils. Under *all* circumstances.'

'Ah yes, the Walton Collection! Do show me where it is. It must be full of books useful to their essay. I'm sure if I asked my pupils to be very careful…'

'Mrs James, am I not making myself clear?'

Henry started. What was he, stupid? Never mind the atmosphere in the gallery, here was a chance to explore he might never get again. Slipping up the stairs, he dived into the recess where Charlie and Meena already crouched, enclosed on all three sides by shelves crammed with ancient-looking books. 'What've you found?' he whispered.

Returning a large, leather-bound book to the shelf and pulling out another, Meena sighed. 'It's all in Latin, with diagrams of stars or something. Looks really boring.'

Henry looked at the rows of thick, dark volumes with their gold lettering: Amicius Boethius, *De Consolatione Philosophiae*; Cornelius Agrippa, *De Occulta Philosophia*; Nicolaus Copernicus, *De Revolutionibus Orbium Coelestium*. The names were unpronounceable, let alone comprehensible. But something inside him flickered.

'So what's so special about these books?' grumbled Charlie. 'You'd think at least there'd be some good pictures. Like skeletons dancing in churchyards, or – or witches being burnt at the stake.' His eyes lit up briefly. 'Some reason for why the place is meant to be haunted. Not just diagrams.'

'Maybe we chose the wrong staircase,' said Meena. 'And the guys over there are having more luck.' She nodded to the recess opposite where Ralph, hands clasped behind his head, sat leaning against the book case, watching Jake and a couple of others plundering the shelves. 'Doesn't look like it though. Or maybe' – a gleam entered her eye – 'it isn't haunted after all. It's just a silly rumour put about by Lavvy to stop us bothering her and her precious Walton Collection. Oh yes, I bet that's it!'

Moving to another shelf, she pulled out a battered volume with no lettering on the cover. 'At last, something in English. Plinie, *The Secrets and Wonders of the Worlde.* Might be interesting.'

Charlie rolled his eyes.

'Wait,' said Henry. 'This is more like it.' He ran his finger down the spine of a tall, slim, newer-looking book bound in black leather, crammed into a space clearly not large enough. '*A History of Northwell School from the Sixteenth Century to the Present,*' he read, 'by Dr Samuel Northwell.' He tugged it out.

Charlie put his head in his hands. 'And just how is that more like it?'

'It's what we need,' whispered Meena, 'for the essay. Oh it *would* have to be in the forbid—'

'How DARE you!'

Meena scrambled to her feet. The group opposite was already up and, led by Ralph, making for the steps down. Henry snapped the book shut and scanned the shelf; the gap had disappeared.

'Just shove it anywhere,' said Charlie. 'Look, there's a space.'

Low, to the right, where Meena had hastily returned the English book, stood about a dozen volumes in faded leather or cloth bindings. No titles on the spines, nothing to indicate their contents, they looked old and worn against the rich covers around them. And yet… a strange feeling stole up Henry's back. It was as if the books' very dullness might conceal more mystery than all the splendid volumes with their diagrams of the stars and planets.

'Hurry *up!*' Charlie urged.

Henry reached out to make a space – and yanked his hand away. A tingling ran through his fingers and up his wrist, as if something warm and alive in there had brushed his skin… *what, a spider?* But it felt more like a human breath.

'What is the *matter* with you?' hissed Charlie.

No choice. No time to make a gap elsewhere. Gripping the *History* hard, Henry pushed it into the shelf. There was something blocking it, soft, resistant, but he couldn't leave the book sticking out half-way! Clenching his teeth he forced it home and recoiled as from the depths of the shelf came a faint sound, like a moan of pain.

Henry didn't breathe. Crouched down, he listened into the darkness, not daring to move his head. It was as if everything around him had been touched by an invisible spark, sending a current zinging from the shelf directly in front of him all round the gallery. No sound, no light; if anything the darkness intensified, and that weird consciousness, that sense of something lurking only just beyond the corner of his eye, returned with a force that froze him to the spot. 'Ch-Charlie,' he whispered.

No reply. Steeling himself, he wrenched his head round to catch Charlie, one hand on the rail, swinging down the steps after Meena. At the turn of the staircase Charlie shot him a grin, mouthing, 'Hurry!' before disappearing from view.

Henry stared. Charlie hadn't felt a thing. Nor had Meena.

Slowly and carefully, he got to his feet. His heart beat more calmly now. Grasping the balustrade, he forced his gaze all round the bookshelves in front of him, then along the gallery, before looking down to the floor below where the rest of his class clustered, sniggering.

Nothing. Still holding the balustrade, he leaned back and closed his eyes. What an idiot, to let the atmosphere up here get to him, all because a book had made a funny sound. Probably the leather binding squeaking slightly as he pressed it into the shelf; that was all. Straightening up, he started down the staircase.

At the bottom stood Mrs D'Arcy, hands splayed on hips. 'You know perfectly well pupils are forbidden to *set foot* on the gallery,' she said. 'What do you *think* you were doing?'

'But Mrs D'Arcy,' Meena opened her dark brown eyes wide. 'Mrs James gave us permission. It's for the Northwell Prize.'

'Mrs James did nothing of the sort, don't lie to—'

'Actually,' the deputy head gave a little cough, 'I *did* tell them they could make full use of the library. *Such* a marvellous opportunity for hands-on research.'

'Hands? *Their* hands? On the Walton Collection?'

The bell went. People rushed for the door, slithering through before either Mrs James or Mrs D'Arcy could break off from their tussle to hold them back.

'Reckon Mrs James has met her match,' said Charlie. 'Old Lavvy'll wipe the floor with her.'

'She's been rumbled though, hasn't she?' said Meena. 'It's just an old library, nothing scary about it at all. Think I might pop in more often now.'

'Three words, Meena,' groaned Charlie. 'Get. A. Life. Hey, Henry, you can let go of the door. There's no one else to come.'

Henry glanced round. This time, he felt *sure*…

But behind him the room lay empty, save for two figures outlined against the window at the far end, deep in argument.

Dropping his arm, he let the heavy oak door click shut.

II

Yes, I saw him. Not the likeliest of subjects, perhaps. Young — not much older than the other by my guess — solidly built but awkward with it; wide, pale eyes, much given to blinking — and the hair! An omen perhaps?

Strange, the workings of fate. Four hundred years and more I have waited for a learned man, a scholar eager for worldly recognition and fame — someone, in short, with whom I can do business — to leaf through these books until he reaches the One. And what do I get? A boy. Another boy.

Yet he may serve my purpose. Two young souls — why should one suspect the other? The second can catch the first and my task will be done.

But I run ahead. As yet he has no inkling of what he has disturbed. It will not do to affright him as I did just now, so overjoyed was I at his discovery! I have held myself back for so long, I can do so a little longer.

The call will come. And I shall be ready.

CHAPTER FIVE

Jacob and Esau

Walton Hall, January 1586

'What? Have you never seen a tapestry before?' On the threshold of the great chamber, Thomas scowled over his shoulder.

'I have,' said John. 'But – not like these.'

After the dim light of the upper corridor, the great chamber felt open and bright, though the sun had long left this side of the house. Warm, too, thanks to the welcome flames burning in fireplaces at opposite sides of the room, above which two gorgeous tapestries faced each other. One showed a carpet of flowers – pale blue, crimson, gold, on a background green as grass, where silken hares bounded and knights and ladies rode horses, falcons on their wrists; while on the other, an ancient, white-bearded figure placed his hand in blind blessing on the bowed head of a young man dressed in furs, as in the distance a hunter emerged from the forest, a deer over his shoulder.

Thomas let out a gasp of impatience. 'Can't you wait

for evening prayers? You'll have leisure enough to gaze your fill then.' Turning right, he disappeared through a doorway.

John hurried after him. So many changes in one day! His mind was filled with the turmoil left behind but one hour since: his mother directing the men carrying chests and hampers into their new home, his sisters running from room to room, marvelling at the space... and then the message from Walton Hall reminding him that *his* new home lay there, no longer with his own family. He swallowed, blinking.

Walking fast, Thomas led the way through another door, stopping at last in a chamber containing a large bed, a plain stone fireplace in which a fire had just been lit, sending strands of warmth into the air, a carved oak chest, and in the far corner near the window, a table with two stools. Waving his hand at the door in the wall opposite, he said, 'My father sleeps through there.'

Silk damask, embroidered in blue and gold, hung from the four bedposts and a coverlet in the same rich fabric lay on the bed, reaching to the floor. John's eyes widened.

Thomas groaned. 'First the tapestries, now the bed. Is it such a marvellous thing to you? Or are you a scullion, accustomed to sleeping on straw?'

No, this was going too far. 'I'm no scullion!' John cried. 'We slept well at Combe too. 'Tis but the degree—'

'The degree?' Thomas let out a harsh laugh. 'Then see this.' Leading John back to the great chamber, he flung open a door on the other side.

Entering the room, John couldn't suppress a gasp. A vast, high bed stood before him, its solid oak posts carved with an intricate pattern of fruit and birds and trailing vine leaves. A frieze of cherubs, their wings tipped with gold, ran round the canopy, at whose corners hung curtains of deep crimson velvet, matching both the coverlet on the bed and the cushions on a great oak chair, carved in a similar pattern to the bed. On the wall opposite, a magnificent marble fireplace lay dark, the grate filled with dried lavender stems; while through the glass in the windows crept the early evening chill.

'Wh-who sleeps here?' he asked. 'Will he not need a fire?'

'She, not he,' said Thomas. 'But no longer. It was my Grandmother Greville's chamber.' He pointed at a picture above the fireplace. 'That's her when she first went to Court. Beautiful, isn't she?'

From the wall Thomas's own dark eyes stared down at John, in the face of a handsome lady in a richly-patterned gown with full sleeves and high collar. Around her throat she wore a double necklace of pearls and rubies, and more pearls were woven into her shining black hair, pulled back under a fine lace cap to emphasise her creamy forehead.

'Very,' he said, dropping his gaze. There was something unsettling in the lady's raised eyebrows and the cold stare that wouldn't release him, no matter where he stood. 'Has she been dead many years?'

'Not dead, fool!' With a burst of laughter, Thomas

gave him a great shove between the shoulder blades. 'She came to live with us after my mother died. Told my father somebody had to see that her grandchild was brought up to know his true worth.' His eyes softened briefly. 'My father was glad enough at the time. But then, three years ago she—' he broke off.

After a moment John ventured, 'Three years ago she –?'

'– left us.' Thomas made for the door, mouth shut tight.

John bit his lip. Here he was, feeling the loss of the family he'd left but a few hours since, and would see again before long – and there was his playfellow still nursing a wound, raw as the day it was dealt! He laid his hand on Thomas's arm. 'You must miss her,' he said.

Thomas jerked the hand away with such force John nearly lost his balance. 'What's it to you?' he hissed, eyes blazing. 'You didn't know her! You *couldn't* know her! If she were here now she'd have found me a more fitting companion – one of my Greville cousins perhaps – than the son of my father's steward!' Striding back through the great chamber he reached his own and hurled himself on to the bed.

John's cheeks burnt as if he'd been struck. Pausing to contain himself, he walked with deliberate step to the foot of Thomas's bed. 'Whatever you may think of me—' he began.

'By your leave, Master John,' said a voice behind him, 'your coffer.'

In the doorway stood a broad-shouldered, ruddy-

41

cheeked figure in dark wool jerkin and breeches, arms clasped round the small leather box that held John's belongings.

'I – that is…' he stammered. *Master* John, was he now? The naming could scarcely come at a worse moment! He stole a glance at Thomas.

But Thomas merely rolled on to the floor and, walking to the oak chest at the foot of the bed, lifted the lid. 'There,' he pointed to a corner. 'You may place your linen. Just see that it doesn't touch mine.'

'Put it down by the chest, if you please,' said John to the man. 'My thanks.'

He jumped as Thomas let the lid fall with a mighty crash. 'Abel is a servant!' he cried. 'He needs no thanks.'

John pressed his lips together. *If that is so I have no wish to be master*, he thought.

His cheerful expression betraying no ill-feeling, Abel bowed. 'Master Thomas,' he said, 'and Master John, I am also to bid you to the great chamber. My master wishes to speak with you before the rest of the household have gathered.'

'Well, why didn't you say so?' Pausing to smooth down his clothes, Thomas pushed past Abel, leaving John to follow in his wake.

Two candelabra had been placed on the long oak table in the middle of the room. Between them a bible lay open and, next to it, a smaller prayer book, ready for the evening devotions. Wearing a fur-lined gown over his doublet and hose, Sir Richard leaned over the table, conferring with his new steward over something John couldn't see; but as he and Thomas entered the room, the master looked up and stretched out his arms. 'Well boys' – and John couldn't suppress a smile at the sheer pleasure filling Sir Richard's voice as he uttered the plural word – 'here you are. What think you, Striven – do they not look like brothers already?'

'By your kindness – they do, sir.'

John looked up to meet his father's gaze. Steady, as ever, but the unusual warmth of his tone made him glow inside. Standing straight, he folded his hands behind his back. This new life might be strange at first; but all would go well.

'Now John, I have something for you.' Turning to the table, Sir Richard picked up what had clearly been occupying his interest before: a small notebook bound in parchment. 'Your father tells me you take pleasure in writing as well as reading. So' – he held it out –'to mark your arrival in Walton Hall, I give you this – to write in whenever and whatever you choose.'

In John's hands the parchment cover felt warm, its clean, leathery fragrance reaching his nostrils. He breathed in deeply. 'Thank you, sir!'

Sir Richard smiled. 'Use it for good, my boy – always for good – and then you cannot go wrong.'

'I will,' John nodded, puzzled. Why would he use it for evil? His eyes met Thomas's and he hastily looked away, clutching his precious gift close to his chest.

'Come, boys.' The half-sleeves of Sir Richard's gown

fell back as he raised his arms. 'My blessing on you both.'

Thomas stepped forward and closed his eyes. Released from their glare, John felt the touch of the warm hand on his head and the murmured words as balm to his soul. Under the master's raised arm he glimpsed a splash of colour: candlelight flickered on the tapestry, illuminating the two main figures, the blind, white-haired old man and the boy kneeling before him, rough goat skins looped over his shoulders and down his arms… *Of course*: *Jacob and Esau*. Jacob stealing his father's blessing while his brother, Esau, looked on from the background, powerless and dispossessed. John had heard the story often enough at church.

Only then did he notice Thomas's dark eyes fixed on the same part of the tapestry and it was as if a chill breeze blew through the room.

Was *that* what his new brother thought?

CHAPTER SIX

Henry's Father Has an Idea

The front door opened slightly and stuck. Bending down, Henry fished out from under it a single shoe with a strap across it, so scuffed it was hard to tell the colour, though the plastic diamonds on the top winked clearly enough.

He pushed the door wide and entered. Hanging his anorak on the peg, he dropped the shoe next to its fellow lying on a bright pink jacket halfway down the corridor. 'Rach!' he yelled.

Straight ahead the kitchen door opened and his sister stood, sticking her tummy out and swinging on the handle. Close to, her face was covered in jam.

'Clear up your stuff,' said Henry. 'One of us'll break our neck.'

Rachel screwed up her face so that all her freckles seemed to join, and tried to beetle her eyebrows, which, while not very bushy, at least could be seen to be there. Unlike his own, so fair they disappeared into his skin altogether. 'Mum says I don't have to,' she said. 'So there.'

'No, I didn't.' His mother appeared in the doorway,

her hair unbrushed and that puffy look around her eyes that showed she'd just woken up. 'I said you could have some tea first, that's what.'

'You're too soft on her, Mum.' Henry went into the back room to put down his bag before returning to the kitchen. From the front room the television rumbled as ever. 'How's Dad?' he asked.

'Oh, you know. Not so bad.'

'Back any better?' As if he didn't know the answer. He poured himself a glass of orange squash.

'Well…' she shrugged.

'Mum.' He took the plunge. 'It's been nearly six months. And it's nothing like as bad as when he first put it out. Can't he get another job? Not a porter's job, something less—'

'No. He can't.' Halfway through wiping Rachel's face with a cloth she whisked round. 'You know that as well as I do! *Now* look what you've done.' Knocked off balance, Rachel fell on the floor. Her face creased up to howl. 'Oh please, can't we just have a nice quiet time together before I go on duty? I have to leave for the hospital at six, I can't be late, there's one nurse off sick as it is, and I haven't got tea sorted yet.'

'I'll help, Mum.' He couldn't bear the tiredness in her voice. 'What're we having – pizza? Yum!' He picked up the box.

'Yes. I've just got to tell your dad what to do – oh come on, Rachel, it's not as bad as that.'

'I think I know how to put a pizza in the oven.'

Behind them and stooping slightly, Dad's huge frame filled the doorway. His shirt was crumpled and the hole in the knee of his tracksuit trousers had got bigger. 'How was the first day back?' he said. 'All right?'

'Fine,' Henry nodded several times.

'Lots of homework?'

'Some. But there's something else, an essay competition. With a prize of twenty pounds!'

It was worth it, for the way his dad's face lit up. 'Go for it, son.' Henry felt an arm – moved carefully, as if its owner didn't quite trust it – round his shoulders. 'You can do it. Never mind the money. But you can show that lot with their fancy clothes and gadgets and smart cars you're as good as they are.'

Rachel snatched something from the work-top. '*I've* got homework. Look, my reading book!'

Dad didn't move. 'In a minute, Rachel.'

'Trouble is,' said Henry, 'it's a history essay and I need to get hold of some books. The school library's no good, you know what Mrs D'Arcy's like and anyway, the one I need is in the Walton Collection which we're not allowed to – why, what's the joke?'

A smile, rare enough these days, hovered on his father's lips. 'Funny that the answer should have occurred to me, of all people, not you,' he said. 'There's a library in town, isn't there?' Shaking his head, he went back to the front room.

Rachel called after him. 'Shall I read it to you later? Dad?' Her voice faltered.

'Rachel, love…' Mum began but Henry was quicker. 'You can read it to me,' he said, bending to look up into her face. '*Please?*'

His sister twirled a strand of coppery hair round her finger. 'All right then,' she sighed, as if doing him a huge favour.

He let the small hand slip into his own, pulling him towards a kitchen chair, while his mind flew to the weekend. The town library! That was a great idea. He'd go on Saturday.

CHAPTER SEVEN

'That Accurs'd Place…'

5 LP

No luck. Not with *A History of Northwell School*, anyway.

Stepping out on to the pavement, Henry pulled the zip of his anorak as high as it would go. OK, so it made him look a geek but around the town library it was unlikely he'd bump into someone from school. And the wind tunnelling through the shopping precinct cut like a knife.

Plunging his hands into his pockets he headed for the bus stop. It hadn't been a complete waste of time. Once he'd worked out, from the local history books, that Northwell School was the same place as Walton Hall, a grand house built about 450 years ago, everything fell into place. The bit of roof holding the funny twisted chimneys and turret, the assembly hall with the loft-thing over the door, the library beyond it with its gallery and all that criss-cross plaster on the ceiling, even the faded old books with no titles on the spines, they all dated from the original building. Made a good starting point for his essay at least, even if he'd have to find the details elsewhere.

But then – he stopped mid-step. That odd footnote in the *County History*. A seventeenth century letter referring to the house as "*that accurs'd place…*" Could that be behind the rumours at Northwell School that the library was haunted? Never mind rumour, was that what he'd felt himself? Somewhere in the darkness of the gallery, among the shelves of old, dusty volumes, there lurked something *evil*?

He shivered. Holding his anorak collar close to his neck, he set off again. Ridiculous. If it really was haunted, Charlie and Meena would've been spooked as well, not just him. But they'd felt nothing. Nor had anyone else. In fact Class 8M's adventure in the library had done a pretty good job of demolishing its scary atmosphere, much to the librarian's disgust. All the same, he'd have given anything to have seen the letter the phrase came from; but, of course, it was in a collection called the Walton Papers, held in the Ancient Records section, and "too fragile" for him to handle. Just his luck.

Clunk. Eyes on the pavement, he collided with a shoulder in a thick cotton sweatshirt. In the same instant, his foot came down on an expensive-looking trainer.

'Ouch! What the hell – *Hamface*! It would be you, wouldn't it!'

Henry leapt back. A dark grey hood loomed over him, a mouth yanked open above a pale, baby-faced chin; all else was in shadow. Behind the figure the glass doors of the games shop opened and closed as people streamed through – oh help, was he in the High Street already? 'J-Jake, I'm sorry, I wasn't looking—' *EH*

'Too right you weren't.' Jake glanced down at his ankle and swore. A patch of mud marked the side of his trainer and leaked on to his sock. The trainers were new.

Henry's mouth went dry. 'It'll come off,' he stammered. 'I-I'll clean it if you like.'

'You'll do that.' The hood nodded slowly. 'Yeah. Maybe I'll make you *lick* the crap away.'

Funny, Jake was being funny. Henry laughed. Then he buckled as pain ripped through his knee. Leaning against the shop front, he held his leg with both hands, while hot tears prickled his eyes. People hurried past, gaze averted.

Jake lowered his foot. 'I wasn't joking.'

'What's going on?' Ralph emerged from the shop, swinging a small plastic bag. Taking one look at Henry, his forehead creased and he turned on Jake. 'What the hell have you been up to?'

'*Me?*' said Jake. 'Nothing. He just barged into me.'

Ralph peered into Henry's face. 'You OK?'

'I-I think so.' Henry tested his leg carefully to see if he could put weight on it.

'Hm,' said Ralph. 'Think you'd better rest that leg.' He looked at him thoughtfully and seemed to make up his mind. 'Tell you what, why don't you come to my place for a bit? We could try out my new game.'

Henry nearly fell over. Ralph Adoney, captain of

football and coolest guy in the school – inviting him round to his house!

A strangled noise came from Jake's throat. From his face he was as staggered as Henry.

The invitation suddenly didn't seem so attractive. 'It's OK,' said Henry. 'You guys have fun. I gotta go.'

'Oh no, Jake can't come,' said Ralph. 'His mum wants him back by two. Gotta catch up on some homework, apparently.' He shot Jake a smile which wasn't returned. 'So that leaves you, me and' – he raised his hand; black, red and white ran together as the shiny plastic bag twirled in the air – '*Death Raven V.*'

'*Death Rav* – you got *that*?' Only the latest computer game, the one everyone was waiting for! Even Charlie, more of an outdoors guy than anything else, had been jabbering about its release for weeks.

With an exclamation of disgust, Jake plunged his hands in his pockets and glared at the ground.

'See you tomorrow, Jake, all right?' Ralph called over his shoulder as, taking Henry's arm, he steered him towards the bus stop.

No reply. Pausing only to give the wall below the shop front a few sharp kicks, Jake finally turned and followed slowly in their wake.

'Won't – won't he mind?' whispered Henry, glancing behind.

'Nah,' said Ralph. 'He'll get over it. Does what he's told. Now forget him' – the bus arrived and he pulled Henry on board – 'I need another player and you need a break. You can't spend all Saturday trawling the library for the Northwell Prize.'

Henry blinked. 'How – how do you know?'

Ralph laughed. 'Henry, you are the biggest geek in the school! Oh, and the rucksack with the A4 pad is a bit of a giveaway.'

CHAPTER EIGHT

At Ralph's

'You live here? What, in all of it?' Henry paused on the gravelled drive to gaze up at the house with its double-gabled roof and wide bay windows either side of the front door. The Fowst family home would fit into this three or four times over.

'Yup.' Ralph grinned and pressed the shiny, round brass bell. 'It's not as big as it looks. Not really.'

The door opened. Ralph's face stiffened and he stood up straight. 'Oh, hi Dad. I thought Mum—'

He broke off as his dad, phone clutched to his ear, motioned him to be quiet. 'Sorry, Steve, just had to answer the door. Don't know where the blazes my wife has got to… you were saying…' Turning, Mr Adoney strode across the hall and disappeared through a doorway.

Ralph gazed after him for a moment. Shrugging his shoulders, he led the way up the wide, pale wood staircase to the first floor and down the passage.

Henry followed, tensing up whenever a step creaked under his foot. 'Is your dad always this busy?' he whispered. 'Every Saturday?'

'Pretty much,' said Ralph. 'You can talk properly by the way. This isn't a museum. Even' – he grimaced – 'if it feels like one. Here we are.' He pushed open a door.

'Wow, Ralph,' said Henry, 'this is awesome.'

Not just because of the football posters on the walls, or the pine bed with built-in shelves stretching across the floor in the far end of the room; it was the fact that Ralph had his own sitting and TV area right here, by the door, with a deep, comfortable sofa, long, low table before it and opposite, the biggest screen Henry had ever seen.

'Yeah,' said Ralph, following Henry's gaze. 'Last year's Christmas present. 'Bout time too, the one I had before was tiny. Dad didn't want me to have it but Mum won him over in the end. Bigger than yours then, is it?'

'Mm.' Henry nodded.

Bigger than his, his parents' and Rachel's put together. Which made perfect sense, given that the only TV at home was in the sitting room for all to watch.

'Oh good, Mum's left me some lunch.' Picking up a plate of sandwiches from the table, Ralph removed the cling film. 'Have some. Smoked salmon.'

Dropping rucksack and coat on the floor, Henry took a sandwich. He bit into it carefully before demolishing it and taking another. 'Mmm,' he said thickly. 'Delicious. Never had this before.'

'You've *never had smoked salmon*?' In the action of returning the plate to the table, Ralph stopped. 'You're missing out there, mate. Get your mum to buy some.'

An awkward silence. Henry found himself staring at a jug and glasses, also on the table.

Ralph put down the plate. 'Apple juice,' he said. 'Help yourself.' Wiping his hands on his jeans, he took the new game out of its bag, ripped off the cellophane and walked over to the Playstation.

Henry poured himself a glass. 'Do you always have lunch like this?' he asked. 'On your own?'

'Not always.' Ralph slid in the disc. 'Mum and I usually eat together but she must've gone out. OK, here goes.' Handing Henry a controller, he grabbed another and launched himself on to the sofa.

'But – what about your dad?'

No reply. Ralph fixed his attention on the screen as '*Death Raven... FIIIIVE,*' came growling from the speakers. The monitor burst into life. Henry tried to concentrate but for a while all he could see was the back of Mr Adoney's head, right elbow akimbo as, phone clamped to his ear, he vanished into his study, too busy even for meals.

Or to greet his own son, standing at the front door.

★

A couple of hours later, Henry sat bolt upright and dropped the controller.

Ralph's eyes didn't leave the screen. '*Yess.*' A few deft shots and Player 2 crumpled into the cave wall. 'Come on,' he said, as the screen froze and reformed, 'you're not giving up?'

'It's not that.' Henry looked at the long sash windows at the far end of the room. Black trees stood out against the darkening sky. 'It's getting late – I gotta go.'

Ralph glanced at his phone. 'Only quarter past five. What's the hurry?'

'A quarter past *five*? Oh no.' Henry lurched off the sofa, slipping on the soft carpet. Shoes, quick, where did he kick them off? 'I should be back by now, my dad'll…' ah, there, in the corner, almost buried in the heap of computer games. A few marbles fell out of his pocket as he bent to put the shoes on; he scooped them up from where they nestled in the thick white pile.

'So text him you'll be late.' Ralph let his controller drop and grabbed a remote off the table in front of him. 'We could watch a DVD.' He waved in the direction of the shelves lining the wall all around the TV screen. 'Choose one.'

Henry paused but only for a moment. 'Can't. My mum's working tonight. Dad needs me to help with Rachel. Anyway,' he added, 'I haven't got a phone.'

'Surely, after all this time, your dad's back must be –' Ralph broke off as if he'd only just heard what Henry said. '*You haven't got a phone?*' He pointed the controls at the monitor, switching it off.

Henry pulled at his trainer straps. The Velcro was old and torn and wouldn't stick. Which was fine, right now. Gave him something to concentrate on.

Ralph gave a low whistle. 'Wow, Henry,' he said. 'I didn't realise. That must be, um, hard. So that's why you're so keen on the Northwell Prize.' He nodded slowly. 'You should win it, too, after all the work you're doing. You deserve it.'

He didn't need to say that! Henry felt his cheeks stretch into a smile he couldn't have controlled if he'd wanted to. 'Thanks, Ralph, that's so—'

'Make your dad happy too, wouldn't it?'

The fizzing in Henry's insides died down. 'Yeah.'

'Well, what's wrong with that?' cried Ralph. 'It's great to have a dad who believes in you. Doesn't just think you're a waste of space.' He stared at his hands hanging loose between his knees.

Henry didn't know what to say. 'Surely—' he mumbled.

'Henry, have you ever seen my dad – before today, I mean? Meeting me at school, or – or watching one of my football matches? No,' Ralph ran on before Henry could reply, 'you won't have done. Because he never comes. Not to a single match. I don't think he'd even know what Northwell School looks like, if it wasn't for the parents' evenings, when he grills every teacher to find out why I'm not top of the class. Or even *near...* not like you.' He shot Henry a sideways glance. 'Wish you could tell me how you do it.'

Henry felt his cheeks go pink. 'Dunno,' he said. 'I – well, like you said, I'm a geek, aren't I? I'd much rather play football like you. That goal you scored against Uplands School last term, from way down the pitch, that was awesome!'

'Yeah,' said Ralph. 'It wasn't bad. Just not good enough for Dad.' Blinking, he looked away before jumping to his feet. 'Come on then, if you've got to go.'

As they descended the stairs, a door opened on the far side of the hall. Henry caught a glimpse of honey-coloured wood and shining granite surfaces before the kitchen door closed again, wafting in a delicious smell of baking, and a slim, fair-haired woman in a soft cream wool dress hurried across the floor. 'Oh, there you are, Ralph. I'm sorry I wasn't here, I forgot some things from the shops. Hallo Jake – oh,' she broke off and smiled. 'It's not!'

'Jake couldn't come,' said Ralph. 'This is Henry. I bumped into him in town.'

'Yes,' said Henry, warming to Mrs Adoney's smile. 'I'd just been to the library and Ralph—'

'Well now, there's a word not often heard in this house,' said a voice behind them. 'The library, eh? Glad to hear that's where my son hangs out these days.' Mr Adoney leaned, arms folded, in the doorway to his study. Without the mobile he looked relaxed, his tanned forehead smooth up to his slightly receding hairline.

A tinge of colour stole up Ralph's cheek. 'Not me, Henry,' he muttered.

'Ah,' said his father. 'I thought it was too good to be true. And I seem to remember your school has an excellent library. Why go to the town one?'

'Because the book I need for the Northwell Prize is in the Walton Collection, which we're not allowed to use,' said Henry, 'and I was hoping to find—'

'The Northwell Prize?' Mr Adoney shot his son a sharp look. 'What's that?'

Ralph closed his eyes. Henry, feeling less and less comfortable by the moment, explained.

'What a marvellous idea!' cried Ralph's mum when he'd finished. 'Malcolm, don't you think?'

Mr Adoney ignored her. 'And you're happy to give up your Saturdays for the chance of winning, what, twenty quid?'

Oh hell, that sounded so sad. Henry nodded.

'See, Ralph?' Mr Adoney swung round to his son. 'That's the spirit I'm talking about! It's not going to be Christmas all your life; you want something, you have to work for it. Like Henry here. Do you understand?'

Henry's cheeks felt burning hot. If only he'd got away before Mr Adoney appeared! Then Ralph wouldn't be standing here in the spotlight, pale-faced, teeth clenched... How he must hate Henry now!

'Yes, Dad.' Ralph looked straight ahead, his blue eyes expressionless.

'Good. Wouldn't do you any harm to have a go at this prize yourself, you know. There could be' – a thoughtful look entered Mr Adoney's eyes – 'more at stake than you think. Well, goodbye, Henry' – he stuck out his hand to shake Henry's – 'nice meeting you. You've given me an idea.' Without another glance at either his son or his wife, he returned to his study.

Mrs Adoney led the way to the front door. Seizing his chance, Henry shot Ralph a whisper. 'Sorry.'

Ralph didn't reply. Something flashed in his eyes – anger? *Hatred*, even? Henry couldn't be sure but it was enough to shake him.

The next moment the look had gone as Ralph gave a shrug of the shoulders and a world-weary smile. 'Don't worry about it,' he said. 'Not your fault.'

'Bye, then, Henry.' Mrs Adoney held the door open. 'Come again, won't you?'

'Thanks, Mrs Adoney,' Henry mumbled. 'Bye, Ralph.'

At the gate, he glanced behind him. In the bay window to the left of the front door stood a familiar figure, one hand on the curtain, gazing out. He waved. Ralph didn't wave back.

Henry had the strangest feeling of that gaze following him all the way down the road, long after Ralph himself had disappeared from view.

CHAPTER NINE

The Gift

The morning light fell grey and cold into the front room. As Henry turned the large, awkward pages, something outside caught his eye. He looked up. From where he sat the small patch of grass in the front garden was invisible; instead, the window seemed to give straight on to the rain-darkened pavement and the line of parked cars masking the road. Nothing unusual there.

'Go on, then. What's next?' Sitting beside him, one arm along the back of the sofa, his dad gave his shoulder a squeeze.

'Sorry, Dad.' Returning to the page, Henry read the first few words – and broke off. There, directly in his line of vision – what the *hell*? Instantly he dropped the newspaper. Mistake. Sheets skidded all over the carpet. If Ralph, standing right outside the window, an odd, half-smile on his face, hadn't noticed before, he certainly would now.

Dad gave an exclamation of annoyance. 'Who's that out there?' He moved a couple of sheets in Henry's direction with his foot. 'Come on, clumsy, pick them up.'

'In a sec, Dad.' Henry raced into the passage, closing the door behind him. *Ralph!* What was he doing? People from school didn't come to his house. Not even Charlie.

'Hi, Henry.' Ralph stood on the doorstep, hands plunged into the pockets of his hoodie. 'Sorry to interrupt your Sunday morning paper reading. Looked nice and cosy in there.'

The familiar heat crept up Henry's neck. *Oh great.* 'Wasn't reading the paper,' he spluttered. 'Not really.'

'Looked like it to me,' said Ralph. 'Out loud, to your dad. Do you read it to your sister, too?'

'No, she only gets bedtime st—' He recollected himself and stopped. 'So, Ralph, you just passing or…?'

'Henry!' The kitchen door banged open behind him. *Oh no.*

'We're going to make a cake later – ooh, hallo.' A scamper of bare feet and Rachel, still in her pyjamas, pushed against his ribs.

Ralph smiled. 'Hello.'

The pressure on Henry's ribs magnified as his sister turned and hid her head against him, while still trying to peep at Ralph. *Shy? Rachel?* 'Go and get dressed,' he hissed, struggling to push her away. *Damn it!* Why was Ralph standing there, taking it all in as if they were some kind of reality TV show?

'Don't have to.' Rachel stuck out her bottom lip. 'It's Sunday. I can stay in my pyjamas all day if I want.'

'Back to the kitchen with you then and get on with

the cake.' He plucked at the surprisingly strong little arms wrapped round his waist. 'Mum's waiting.'

'No she isn't, silly,' she gurgled. 'Mum's gone to bed now. We're going to make it *after.* And she wants you to go and get some baking powder. Dad was meant to buy some yesterday but they've changed the packing and he got bicarb— Ow! Henry!'

Gurgling erupted into a wail as he forced her arms apart and pushed her back roughly down the passage. Too roughly but right now he didn't care. 'Just get lost!' he yelled. OK, so now he was really and truly in for it but too bad. He must see what Ralph wanted and steer him away.

Stepping out of the house, he pulled the front door to. 'Sorry, Ralph,' he muttered, walking him to the gate.

'No worries. Your sister's sweet.'

Henry blew a long breath into the icy air. *Yeah. Right.*

'Anyway, I just called round to say sorry about yesterday. My dad putting you on the spot like that. And I thought you might like this.' Taking something out of his pocket, he gave it to Henry. 'I don't need it anymore, now I've got a new one.'

Henry blinked. In his hand lay a mobile phone. He opened his mouth to speak but nothing came out.

'Here's the charger.' Ralph dropped it into his other hand. The wire slipped though his fingers but he barely noticed. 'There's a couple of quid left on it so you won't have to top it up for a bit.'

'Ralph.' Henry's voice felt hoarse. 'Are you – are you sure?'

''Course. It'll only get thrown away otherwise. And I'll tell you something else I'm sure about.' Thrusting his hands back in his pockets, he looked Henry straight in the eye. 'You are going to win that prize. If anyone deserves to, you do, and I want to help.'

'Wow – thanks, Ralph, that's great but…' Shouldn't Ralph be entering himself, like Mr Adoney said?

A smart rap came from the window behind him. Turning, he saw Dad mouthing through the glass, Rachel's tearful face beside him. Swivelling back, he was puzzled to catch Ralph gazing in the same direction, an odd, almost hungry look on his face.

The next moment it had gone and Ralph's lips twisted into a half-smile. 'Look. I know what you're thinking,' he said. 'But whatever my dad says, it's not me. Sure, I could have a crack at the prize but I wouldn't win so why waste my time? I'd be much happier if you won it. In fact' – his eyes gleamed – 'I've been trying to work out how you can get the book you need from the Walton Collection. I reckon you're just going to have to borrow it.'

Henry's mind reeled as he tried to keep up with Ralph's train of thought. 'Borrow?' he echoed. 'Not possible. You know that.'

'I'll help you.' Leaning against the low garden wall, Ralph folded his arms. 'I'm pretty good at distracting Lavvy. You could sneak up and get it.'

'But – we could get into trouble,' Henry stammered. 'And wouldn't it be kind of like – well – cheating?'

Ralph shrugged. 'How can it be cheating when you're just getting the best book for the job? It's not your fault it's in the wrong part of the library.'

That was so true! And reaching it would be a matter of moments, Henry could see it already: the stairs leading up to the gallery, his hand running along the faded spines until – until… the memory flooded back and he shuddered.

'Monday lunchtime, OK? Unless – hey, you're not *scared* of the place, are you?'

Henry blinked. ''C-course not.' There was nothing there! He'd imagined it – that was all. And as Ralph said, how else was he to find out anything about the school? He'd borrow the book, look after it carefully and return it. Where was the problem?

'Great.' Ralph smiled. 'See you then.' He set off down the street.

Slipping the precious phone into his pocket, Henry gazed after the retreating figure, trying to quell the fizzing inside him. Ralph Adoney was on his side; he was going to help him win!

The front door opened. 'Henry!' cried his dad. 'Come here *this minute*!'

CHAPTER TEN

Ralph Keeps His Promise

'… just awesome, it's set in this massive cave world and everything you see you can manipulate and you can get special gifts by shape shifting, like if you get close to a cat, suddenly you've got night vision.' Reaching the playground, Henry paused to draw breath.

'Yeah.' Charlie's attention was on the football pitch. Some distance away, groups of players were snatching a quick game before school.

Henry faltered. This was odd. One minute Charlie couldn't stop talking about *Death Raven V*, the next, he'd lost interest. ''Course, I didn't get very far,' he ploughed on, 'but Ralph says I can come back any time—'

'Ralph!' Charlie swung round. 'How come he's your new best mate all of a sudden? You told me you had no time to play football on Saturday 'cause you were going to the library. Looks like you had some spare time after all.'

'It – it just happened,' Henry stammered. 'I didn't know I'd be – oh, come on, Charlie, it's no big deal, is it? I mean,' he corrected himself, 'I'm sorry.'

Charlie nodded slowly, staring at the ground.

Henry groaned inside. 'Play you in lunch today – if you want to, that is.' Too late he remembered. He slammed his fist against his brow.

'What?' said Charlie.

'Um – I mean not today, tomorrow maybe?'

A look of wariness entered Charlie's face. Bang on cue, a beeping sound came from Henry's left pocket.

The wary look vanished. Charlie's freckles stretched into an expression of utter amazement. 'You've got a *phone*?'

Heat rushed up Henry's neck. Oh hell, this was getting worse. 'Ralph – he didn't need it anymore.' Fishing out the phone, he jabbed his fingers on the keys.

'Hi, there. You got my text then.' School bag hanging loosely over his shoulder, Ralph stood at the mouth of the tunnel between the dining room and music blocks. The stream of people pouring through had to part on either side of him.

'Yup,' Henry nodded. 'Got it. All fine.'

'Good. See you then. Don't be late.' Ralph strolled away.

'Sure.' Henry's neck began to ache. What an idiot he must look, nodding away like this! 'Er, Charlie, you're probably wondering – Charlie?'

The space next to him was empty. Charlie was halfway across the playground, zigzagging between the clusters of people. He didn't look back.

★

Ralph entered first. Striding down the long room, one hand in his pocket, he looked completely at ease, as if he did this kind of thing every day of his life. While Henry, heart beating in his ears, squatted up against the stone mouldings behind the half-open door, hastily pulling off his shoes. On a sudden thought he drew his marble bag from his pocket and placed it on top of them.

'Hallo, Mrs D'Arcy. How are you?'

A creak as the librarian relaxed into her chair. 'Very well, thank you, Ralph. How kind of you to ask.'

Ralph was clearly working his charm. From the sound of her voice, Mrs D'Arcy had tilted her head to look straight up at him, and with luck he could hold her there for a moment. Keeping the tall figure directly between him and the librarian, Henry crept through the door to the bottom of the right-hand staircase and crouched behind it. So far, so good.

'And what can I do for you, Ralph?'

'Well, Mrs D'Arcy, I know how busy you are, but – '

Careful, Ralph, thought Henry. *Don't overdo it.*

'– could you show me the local history section? It's for the Northwell Prize.'

'Of course.' The gracious tone broadened into a smile marked by the sound of lipstick cracking. 'It's just over there.'

'Oh, *thank* you, Mrs D'Arcy, you're *such* a help.'

'Don't mention it. My pleasure.'

On second thoughts, don't worry. Overdoing it is not possible.

Ralph walked over to the left-hand of the two book stacks occupying the floor in that end of the room. Henry held his breath.

'Mrs D'Arcy, I'm really sorry but I can't seem to find anything.'

'Oh, you boys,' the librarian heaved a sigh. 'Wait, I'll show you.'

Henry's heart thumped. This was his moment. Chair legs scraped, followed by the *click click* of stilettos and then the sound of a stiff dress creaking as Mrs D'Arcy crouched down behind the book stack. Now. *Now.* Round the bottom of the stairs, a few steps up – he hesitated.

At the top the recess lay swathed in darkness. Well, so what? Why couldn't he rid himself of the feeling that something lay concealed there, watching, waiting... *that accurs'd place.* He whisked round. An echo in his mind, he knew; yet it sounded as if someone had spoken the words out loud.

He gripped the step above him with both hands. *Don't be an idiot*, he told himself. *There's nothing – no one – there.* Setting his teeth, he pushed himself to the top of the staircase, into the recess and sank to his knees.

'Look, Ralph, down here. See? Now this one would be perfect.'

Cold. Like ice hanging in the air. And such sadness – where did that come from? The darkness seemed to gather round him, pressing him on all sides, weighing him down so that he huddled on the floorboards, palms flat, shoulders hunched, unable to move. What had happened in this place? More to the point – what was happening to him? This was crazy! He was there to get a book. Was that so hard? He forced his gaze up to look along the shelves. Rectangular shapes, grey, faded yellow, black… Black, that was it! The tall, slim volume with gold lettering on the spine, less faded and battered than the others, near the right-hand corner of the recess. All he had to do was reach towards it, ease it out…

He snatched his hand back. What *was* that – an electric shock? It couldn't be. Pins and needles, probably, from crouching down in this cramped space. He tried again, pressing hard through the sparky feeling until he'd drawn the book out and tucked it under his sweatshirt, vaguely aware of something odd about its shape. It felt thicker than it should, and uneven.

From the book stack below came the sound of Ralph rising to his feet. 'Thanks, Mrs D'Arcy. It's just what I need.'

'You're very welcome, Ralph.'

Cold sweat ran down Henry's back. He'd got what he wanted; now for the staircase down. At the first step he glanced behind him and stifled a scream.

Eyes, red as fire, stared at him from the darkness of the gallery.

He launched himself at the stairs. Half slipping, half sliding, he reached the bottom and knelt there, heart bursting in his chest, awaiting Lavvy's cry of outrage. At that moment he didn't care who saw or heard him, all that mattered was to get the hell out of there and never come back.

The cry didn't come. Instead, the calm clicking of stilettos in the opposite direction told him the librarian was returning to her desk. Pausing just long enough for his breathing to die down, Henry crept across the floor and out of the library.

III

Go, friend. You have your prize. Not long now and your prize will deliver mine.

Ah, but the waiting! To have you so close, within touching distance – had I the means to touch – is it any wonder that my resolve should waver, giving you a glimpse of what it were better you did not see?

But fear not. Once summoned into living, breathing shape, I leave all that behind, bringing with me only zeal to do your bidding to the best of my powers.

It is not too much to ask you to serve me in return.

★

Out in the corridor Henry's legs gave way. He sat, head between his knees, while images of what he'd just seen tumbled through his mind.

What had he seen? Or rather, thought he'd seen? Because there wasn't – couldn't have been anyone there, let alone someone with red eyes! Unless it was a rat (did

Northwell School have rats?). No, not big enough. A cat, then. But how would it get into the library? And where was the light – he shivered – that could have given its eyes that fiery glow?

Sitting up, he put on his shoes and got to his feet. Not a good idea to be sprawling here for the head to find on the way to his office. Reaching for his marble bag, he let its solid, familiar shape weigh in his hand and his face relaxed into a smile. Here was something real and tangible, not a product of his imagination. In the darkness of the gallery he'd let his mind play tricks on him, yet again. Whatever he'd seen, there'd be a simple explanation; pieces of coloured glass decorating a book binding, perhaps. Only his nerves, stretched tight by the whole secrecy thing, had turned it into something else.

And he'd got the book! All that remained was to hide it safely. Stuffing the marble bag back in his pocket, he made for the playground. Across the tarmac, through the swing door, up the stairs to his classroom – here was a stroke of luck. The place was empty. Sliding the book out from under his sweatshirt into his school bag, he headed back outside.

Ah, so that's where everyone had got to. There, on the far side of the playground, where tarmac met grass rolling down towards the football pitch, a swarm of people clustered round the notice board. They craned over each other's shoulders to get a better look before falling back, stamping their feet with cold and chattering excitedly.

Henry quickened his step. It looked like the team lists had been put up and, OK, he wasn't a cert like Charlie but you never knew…

Drawing near, he hesitated. This was odd. Football notices didn't usually arouse such interest from the girls. He ducked as a pair of long black plaits whisked round.

'Henry, have you seen this?' said Meena.

'Doesn't need to, does he?' Charlie's glance went over Henry's head as he pushed past. 'Knows about it already.'

Henry grabbed his arm. 'What? What do I know?'

'Your new friend's told you, hasn't he?'

'What new friend?' said Meena.

Henry's heart swelled in his chest. 'You mean I'm in?' he cried. 'Wow, no, Ralph didn't tell me! Guess I'm not so bad at football after all!' He gave Charlie a sidelong grin.

Meena looked puzzled. 'What's football got to do with it?'

Charlie sighed. 'Not football, stupid. Just look at the board.' Extracting his arm from Henry's, he walked away.

CHAPTER ELEVEN

The Price

The Northwell Prize for Year 8
I am delighted to announce that for this year only,
the winner of this competition will receive,
in addition to the £20 prize money,
A LAPTOP
supplied by Adoney Computers plc.
By kind donation of Mr Malcolm Adoney.

Alistair Robertson
Headmaster

Henry stared at the notice board in disbelief. A *laptop*!
He'd have done it for twenty quid, for nothing even,
just for his dad – but this changed everything!

And Mr Adoney – what made him do this? He didn't
even know about the prize before Saturday evening.
Henry's mind flew back to the tall, relaxed figure in
open-necked shirt and chinos who'd fixed him with a
penetrating gaze as he'd stammered out the details; then
the handshake and *Goodbye, Henry… You've given me an*

idea. Was *this* what it was? To make the prize a much bigger deal – did he hope that way to tempt his own son to enter?

Maybe. In which case – poor Ralph! He must be kicking himself now. Forced to choose between a smartphone and a laptop for Christmas (oh, to have his problems!), he couldn't have known what his father had in mind or he'd never have helped Henry get the book. Well, he could have Dr Northwell's *History* after Henry, that was only fair. Though quite amusing, too, when you thought about it.

'Knew you'd be pleased,' said Meena. 'I bet everyone'll have a go now. Mrs James must be over the moon.'

'Yeah,' said Henry.

The events of the last twenty-four hours flashed through his brain as he retraced his steps across the playground. What a stroke of luck this notice hadn't appeared earlier in the day and caused Ralph to call off the whole library venture! As it was, everything was working like a dream.

★

Several hours later, Henry threw himself down on to his bed, reached for the pillow and plumped it against the wall behind him. From the bathroom came splashing and snatches of singing – '*She's the top – she's fantastic – she's the strongest, she's the smartest, Rachel FOWWWST!*'

Good. Rachel's bath would last some time yet. He should be safe for a while.

Opening his school bag, he hesitated, bracing himself for – for what? It was just a book! Drawing it out, he felt no trace of the tingling that had rippled through his fingers when he'd pulled it from the shelf. Which made perfect sense. His hand had gone to sleep in the gallery, that was all; came of working himself up so much, just because of a bit of darkness!

All the same, the book felt odd: soft, not hard, on its underside. The memory of something spongy in the shelf pushing against his hand came back and his stomach rose. Slowly he turned the book over.

He nearly laughed out loud. Another flat shape – slight, like an exercise book, with a yellowing cover made of a material stronger yet suppler than paper – had stuck to Dr Northwell's. That was what had been resisting him! It must have got in the way when he'd thrust the *History* into the shelf.

Carefully peeling the books apart, he dropped the stowaway on the bed beside him before opening *A History of Northwood School*. In thin, seriffed capitals, the title expanded to include *"formerly Walton Hall, from 1564 until the Present Day"*, with *"London, 1898"* printed at the bottom. Opposite, a grey and white photograph showed a stern, craggy-faced gentleman with long white whiskers, wearing a black gown over his suit and waistcoat. Henry sighed. The founder of Northwell School didn't look a bundle of fun. Nor, by the thick lines of print that greeted him as he leafed through, did his style of writing.

Never mind. He'd skim what he could. At least some pages were given over to photographs or old-fashioned illustrations, the kind where lots of fine lines made up the shading. One of these showed the long frontage of a grand house, formed into an "H" shape by wings running at right angles at either end. *"Walton Hall, southern aspect, as it might have appeared in 1568,"* read the caption, and Henry studied it carefully. This was looking from the far side of the main school building, the old entrance on the busy road, used until the erection of the music and dining room blocks to the north created a quieter way in.

He raised his eyebrows. Walton Hall had been some house. An in-and-out pattern of bay windows two storeys high, one corner of each wing ending in a great hexagonal tower that reached up as if they were so many corners of a castle; and on the roof – ah, he recognised those! Tall, spiral-patterned chimneys, not just one pair but dozens, placed at intervals along all three stretches of roof, with here and there a little domed turret.

Henry smiled. So here was the reason for the library's great age – and the assembly hall's too, by its matching long windows – they were all that remained of the original Walton Hall. A jumble of Victorian brick and modern glass and concrete blocks accounted for the rest of Northwell School.

Something hummed near his leg. He jumped and fumbled in his pocket. *Your phone, duh.*

'Hi, Ralph. What's up?'

'Hi, Henry. Just wondering if you've seen the notice.'

'You bet I have!' Henry bounced to a more comfortable position to talk. 'Isn't it great? Must have been a shock for you though – I guess your dad wanted to surprise you as much as everyone else.'

A soft laugh at the other end of the line. 'Not quite.'

'You mean, you *knew*? And you still wanted to help me – not try for it yourself? Wow, Ralph, that's really nice of you.'

'Yeah. I'm glad you think so because now I need to ask you a favour.'

'Sure!' cried Henry. 'Anyth—'

'Good. I want you to write the essay for me.'

'What?' Henry laughed. He'd misheard, right?

'The Northwell essay,' Ralph repeated, his voice calm and friendly as before. 'Do the best job you can, pass it over to me – unnamed, of course – and I'll give it in. OK?'

Henry gripped a handful of duvet to steady himself. It was the only part of his body that moved.

'Oy, you still there? I said—'

Henry felt as if his throat was sticking together. Licking his lips, he tried to swallow. 'Ralph, you – you can't mean that. It wouldn't be right.'

'Can't I? I'll tell you what's not right.' The warm tone vanished. Ralph's words came out hard and fast. 'It isn't right that you come round to my place and show me up in front of my dad—'

'Ralph, I didn't mean—'

'– blabbing away about how you just love spending your free time working your socks off in the library—'

'I never said that, I only— '

'– playing to my dad's favourite "you've got to work for what you want" obsession—'

'Ralph, I'm really sorry that happened.'

'So now it's payback time, see? I'm going to beat my dad at his own game. And you're going to help me.'

'Look, Ralph' – Henry fought to make his voice work properly – 'I can't do that. You know I can't. You've been really great with the book and all, and thanks for lending me your phone but it's OK, I don't need it. I'll give it back to you tomorrow.'

'No, you'll keep it. I'll be wanting to check up on how you're getting on.'

Rachel had stopped singing. From the strong sucking noise and rushing of water through pipes the bath plug was out. In a few minutes she'd come charging in, hair dripping and pyjamas half on.

Henry bent forward, clutching the mobile to his ear. 'I told you, I can't do your essay as well as mine. It'd be – well – cheating. Sorry.'

That was dangerous; tantamount to a direct accusation. He braced himself for the reaction.

Ralph sniggered. 'Cheating? This from someone

who's stolen a valuable library book so he can use it and no one else?'

Henry's heart stood still. The mobile fell from his hand. When he lifted it back to his ear he had to grip tight to stop the trembling. 'Not – not stolen,' he whispered. From the other side of the wall came the sound of bare feet squeaking on linoleum. He must get through this and fast. 'I borrowed it, *you* know that. It – it was your idea.'

'*My* idea? How do you make that out? All I did was ask Mrs D'Arcy to show me the history section. I didn't know what was going on behind me. Not going to look good when I tell her – and the head, given how serious this is – that you're a thief.'

Henry wrenched his mouth open but the words jammed in his throat. A hot stinging rushed behind his eyes.

'So here's your choice, Hamface. Be nice and do what I ask – and you sure as hell owe me – or you're looking at a criminal record. You can write another essay to enter as your own, of course: I realise your *dad*' – he stretched out the sneer – 'will expect it. Just make sure you remember which is the one that matters.'

'R-Ralph, p-*please*— '

'Oh, and one more thing. Don't try anything funny. Like sneaking the book back, for instance. Because then I really would have to tell them. And, let's see, whose word would count for more? My dad's really generous, you know. Really supportive of the school. Don't think the head will want to upset him, do you? Besides, with your *hamface*' – he paused. In the silence that followed his grin was almost audible.

The heat flooded up Henry's neck. From somewhere high up in his throat a cry broke.

'Yeah.' Ralph's voice dripped like honey down the phone. ''S'what I meant. Good luck with trying to deny it. See you tomorrow.'

CHAPTER TWELVE

In the Maze

Shoulders hunched against the wind, Henry walked across the playground. Nobody bothered him. Perhaps because he looked as if he had somewhere to go, something urgent to do. That was certainly the idea. Or because most of Year Eight were using the lunch hour to research in the library, as had been the pattern for the last four days. Mrs D'Arcy must be going spare.

Four days. During which time he'd hardly slept, hadn't heard what was going on around him, snapped at Rachel and been yelled at by Dad; while Mum, seeing the dark circles round his eyes, intervened, a troubled look entering her own which made everything so much worse – but what could he do?

Think it through, that's what. There must be a way out. What he needed was somewhere safe, not just from his enemies – funny how Ralph managed to hang around with Jake and yet still be always at his shoulder – but even from his friends. 'Not going to the library *at all*, Henry?' Meena had asked him, heading there straight from lunch. He'd ducked and mumbled something before hurrying away.

The library. He never wanted to enter it again.

Long grass on the edge of the games field soaked through the splits in his shoe leather. But at least this way he avoided the kids playing football. A quick glance assured him that Charlie wasn't among them. Probably ransacking the bookshelves, even him. He smiled, in spite of himself. Amazing what the lure of a laptop could do.

Rising up ahead, the tall stone war memorial marked where the ground fell away towards the river; to the right, a thicket of trees and bushes, willow and ash and hawthorn, offered shelter. Ralph was hardly going to leg it all the way over here.

No, but the phone! He dived his hand into his pocket and pulled it out. Off, of course, for lessons. *Phew*. He wasn't going to turn it on now, or ever, if he could help it; but Ralph had already seen to that. It was Henry's choice, he'd hissed down the landline last night. Did he want his dad to be bothered every evening? So switch on the mobile. It was unbelievable! He might just as well be tagged!

Flinging his back against a tree, Henry stared through a lattice of thin, bare branches at the black water winding its way between the banks. Weed-infested, the river. If you fell in, the weeds would wrap tendrils round your ankles and before you knew it you'd be so entangled you'd drown.

So entangled… Henry closed his eyes.

When did Ralph go from seeing him as someone to play computer games with to a weapon he could use in the war against his father? Did he ask him round in the first place to impress his dad – *see, I have geeks for friends, too, not just thugs like Jake* – only to hate him when the plan backfired? If only Henry'd kept his mouth shut! If he hadn't mentioned the Northwell Prize none of this would have happened.

Gusts of wind ruffled the surface of the water. Henry groaned. Useless to keep going over it; he was here now. What were his options? Defy Ralph and return the book? He'd be shopped on the spot. Keep it till he'd read what he needed, slip it back into the library and quietly hand in his essay? Yeah, brilliant. Exposure in front of the whole school when Ralph found out. Because how else to account for where he got all his information? *You should have thought about that before,* said a small voice inside his head. *Instead of letting Ralph's clever plan carry you away.*

People were leaving the games field; he'd better trek back. To hell with the laptop, the money, the lot. He'd do what Ralph wanted. Something echoed in his mind and for a second he was back in the high street, watching a figure with spiky yellow hair glare silently at him from under his hooded sweatshirt while Ralph, laughing, assured him he had nothing to worry about. *Jake does what he's told.* Yeah. Ralph liked that in a person.

Stepping from the wet grass on to the playground, Henry found his way barred by a figure standing with her arms folded across her chest.

'*There* you are, Henry! What is with you, spending the

whole of lunch break by the river? Do you *want* everyone to think you're a complete loner?'

It was like having another sister. Two Rachels bossing you around, one at school and one at home. Heck, what a thought. 'None of your business, Meena, if I feel like a bit of fresh air instead of—' he broke off. 'Where did you get that?'

From inside her folded arms the top half of a book peeped out. It was large and black with gold lettering on the front.

Like the one sitting on his desk at home.

'See what you're missing?' She grinned. 'From the library, of course. The one in the Walton Collection's a first edition; it's been reprinted and the history section's got six copies. You should've seen Lavvy's face when we all charged in there, asking for stuff about the school. She *so* didn't want to show us but – what's wrong?'

The history section. Where Ralph decoyed Mrs D'Arcy. He knew about the modern copies all the time.

Meena took a step back. 'Look, you – you can have it as soon as I've finished,' she said. 'I'll be quick as I can.'

'Huh?' Henry shook himself. 'Sorry, Meena. I – yeah, that would be great. Thanks.'

'OK.' With a nod, she headed for the classroom block, her tight black plaits shining in the cold sun.

Henry stared after her. Why was he working himself up like this? It mightn't be either him or Ralph who won the Northwell Prize.

It might be Meena.

CHAPTER THIRTEEN

The Curse of John Striven

Pushing open his bedroom door, Henry glanced at the alarm clock by the bed. Ten past two. Perfect. The afternoon session at the swimming pool went on till half past four on Saturdays and, knowing Rachel, she'd keep Dad there till the bitter end. A couple of hours of peace, at least.

The old side table that served as his desk creaked as he sat down in the chair. Sweeping aside marbles, pens, comics, swap cards and half-eaten packets of sweets, he dragged the book to the centre and opened it.

"In 1564, Sir Richard Walton, a scholar whose interest in the new humanist learning had won him the patronage of Queen Elizabeth I, left the Court at Whitehall with enough wealth to build himself a splendid family seat."

He built a *seat*?

Henry sighed. This looked to be a heavy read. But who cared? After the last few days, it felt light as anything, thanks to Meena.

A huge weight had slipped from his shoulders. Because if everyone else was using Dr Northwell's *History*, then so could he. No one could trip him up over knowledge he wasn't supposed to have. On Monday he'd slip this copy back into the library – any shelf would do – borrow Meena's and tell Ralph to get lost. Yeah, he'd been a complete idiot. But it was over now.

So, to the building of Walton Hall. The east wing contained a study and parlours with bed chambers above, also the great chamber – a kind of family room where the household met for meals and prayers. The west wing held the kitchen, main staircase and a couple of other large rooms. In the middle, taking up both floors, lay the hall and next to it, the library, which was unusual in having a gallery, possibly the only one in England at that time. OK, this was useful but not exactly history… He let his eye run down the page.

Ah, this was more like it.

"In 1646, a siege by the Parliamentarians in the Civil War ended in a conflagration that destroyed all but the hall and library: a pattern of almost total destruction by fire that recurred several times during the following centuries.

Doubtless this unfortunate tendency of Walton Hall's to go up in flames lies at the root of the legend of the Curse of John Striven. The embittered foster-son of Sir Richard Walton, he is said to have vowed revenge at being excluded from his foster-father's will."

There it was. *That accurs'd place* – an echo of the footnote in the *County History*! Had he just found the source of the haunting rumours? Some ancient malevolence left hanging in the air, long after its origins had been forgotten?

Henry's heartbeat quickened. The Northwell Prize essay looked like being more exciting than he thought. More exciting and more... scary. The darkness up in the library gallery, the sudden chill, the eyes watching him...

No! Sitting back in his chair, Henry folded his arms. He'd imagined all that. There was nothing there. How could there be, hundreds of years later? The house didn't even exist anymore.

Except that it did. The heart of it, perfectly preserved, was now the heart of Northwell School. The old library with its valuable collection of books held in a gallery where no one set foot – that had probably hardly changed since Sir Richard's day. Something could be lying there, undisturbed, just waiting for the step on the stair, the crack in the silence that would wake it from centuries of sleep...

Henry closed his eyes so tightly he could feel the muscles ache. That was rubbish, stupid, superstitious rubbish! Of course people had been in the gallery down the years: Dr Northwell, for a start. From the way he wrote he didn't set much store by the house's legendary reputation. It hadn't put him off turning it into a school, which, as far as Henry could tell, had survived pretty well ever since.

"I am inclined to ascribe the legend to Sir Richard's own reputation as a collector of manuscripts on alchemy and magical arts, subjects at the time deemed worthy of a natural philosopher's interest, but which may well have allowed an atmosphere of mystery to gather around Walton Hall in subsequent years."

Henry sucked in his breath. Sir Richard collected *magical* books! Those old volumes in the library full of maths diagrams with Latin explanations… perhaps they weren't as dull as they looked. That strange feeling hovering at the back of his mind, somewhere between excitement and fear, rushed forward again and he fought it back with all his strength. He was writing a history essay, for goodness' sake; facts were needed – not rumours and atmospheres!

This John Striven, for instance; he sounded interesting. Henry's eye returned to the page.

"However, my researches reveal that a John Striven did indeed exist in the household, though little beyond that fact. Account books for the period (largely complete, save for a puzzling three-year gap in the late 1580s) name Sir Richard's steward as one Edward Striven, and there is a reference in 1586 to his son John's being brought into the household as a companion for twelve-year-old Thomas Walton, a practice not uncommon at the time."

Account books for the period – wait, that soft pamphlet thing that had stuck itself to Dr Northwell's *History* looked like an account book. Shuffling through the pile of comics, Henry fished it out.

It was an account book all right, but not the kind with figures. More like a diary. It looked old, much older than Dr Northwell's book. Written in faded brown ink on yellowing paper, the spelling strange and some of the letters finishing in loops and curls, the words were still readable, as if formed by a not yet very confident hand.

A date headed the first page. Not just any date.

The book trembled in his hands. Putting it down, he picked up the *History* again and checked.

This was extraordinary.

"Monday, thise 20th day of Januarie, 1586

It is fittinge that thise boke, given mee, John Striven, but one hour since by my Master, sholde bear Witnesse to the great Change in my Life that His Kindnesse hath wrought. His Goodnesse in taking mee into his Householde as Companion to Master Thomas is beyond Measure. Surelie I will soon grow Accustom'd to my new Playfellowe and if I acquit myselfe well, be enroll'd in the University with him, where I may make that Studie of Natural Philosophie I long to doe."

The embittered foster-son! This was his diary! Dr Northwell couldn't find out anything about him, yet here, in his own library, lay – Henry flipped through the pages – a whole year's worth of information. How did the doctor miss it?

He didn't know it was there. Slipped behind those shabby, unmarked books, it had lain hidden until – until his own clumsy hand, panicking, had thrust Dr Northwell's *History* against it so hard he'd crushed the smaller book against the larger one.

Coldness stole down Henry's limbs. Supposing – just *supposing* there was something in this legend business. That John Striven really had cursed Walton Hall so that large parts of it burnt down, not once but several times; could his diary, disturbed after centuries of lying forgotten, reawaken that curse? In which case, he, Henry, had done just that! What if, he turned up at school tomorrow to find it in flames?

With a groan Henry slumped in his chair. *Get a grip.* It was just a diary. A bundle of old paper could scarcely set a building on fire. Not unless someone put a match to it and lobbed it through a window. Yeah, that would work.

Leaning back he raised both arms and stretched. There he was, getting into a state, when he should be shouting for joy at this chance to be the first person in four hundred years to read a diary never discovered before! All these rumours of a curse only made it more interesting, nothing else.

Nothing else. Biting the inside of his cheek, he began to read.

CHAPTER FOURTEEN

A Day in the Life of John Striven

Walton Hall, January 1586

Here was a difference indeed! Instead of sitting crammed on to one long, rickety form with a dozen school fellows, waiting his turn to construe his lesson, John had for himself the whole of one side of a wide table, with plenty of room for books, paper, pen and ink. Opposite, Thomas's eyes were so narrow it was hard to read their expression; though the twist of his closed mouth was plain enough. From time to time it burst open in a sharp laugh at John's stumbling: as well it might, for there was no getting his tongue round these outlandish French sounds, for all the patience with which Doctor Thorne repeated them, seated at the head of the table.

At last the French hour ended and John's spirits lifted. For now came Latin; and in that he should not disgrace himself. And indeed, half-way through translating a passage from Ovid's *Metamorphoses*, he felt the touch of a hand on his arm.

'A fine piece of work, Master John,' said Dr Thorne. 'Master Thomas, your new playfellow will put you on your mettle, I think. Continue, if you please.'

The smile in the doctor's watery eyes sent a warm glow through John's heart. He sat up straight, waiting for Thomas to complete the lines still ringing in his own brain.

Thomas scowled down at his book. His right hand resting on the table curled, as if gripping an invisible sword. Watching him, John felt the tide filling his chest ebb and melt away.

Eleven o'clock came: the hour to present themselves in the great chamber for dinner. Yet the churning in John's stomach was such that he could barely eat a morsel of all the fine meats and dishes served on silver platters on the great oak buffet.

'I see your son will be no burden on us, Striven,' said Sir Richard, slicing into a piece of venison on his trencher and giving John a large wink. 'Though I fear what his mother would say should we let him starve.'

'I pray he may be no burden, sir,' came the reply. John glanced at his father, sitting at Sir Richard's right hand: a smile he could not hope for, but a look at least? A slight nod, a lift of the eyebrow – and his father's attention rested on the master once more. Still, that was something.

'Come, John,' said Sir Richard, 'you must eat. Abel will carve you some mutton.'

Standing at his master's shoulder, Abel grinned and

walked over to the buffet. Some deft knife work and a juicy piece of meat – not too large, thankfully – lay on John's trencher. A delicious aroma curled upwards.

'What fare is it you are accustome'd to, pray?' asked Thomas. 'Carrots?' His gaze rose pointedly to rest just above John's forehead.

John's hand paused halfway to his lips. He lowered it and looked downwards, feeling the heat stealing up his neck.

Sir Richard glared at his son. 'Keep a civil tongue, sirrah! I'll not have you mock your companion thus.'

Thomas bowed his head. 'Cry you pardon, John,' he said.

John forced himself to meet those cool eyes. In their depths he saw reflected the flame in his cheeks, as bright as his hair.

Evening came at last and never had John felt so glad to enter his chamber and fall on the bed. Four more hours of study – Latin and French, but also Cosmography (good) and Accounting (that he could well have done without) – had at least woken his appetite and he'd been able to do better justice to supper than to dinner, to his master's evident delight. Thomas, too, had shown greater friendliness than he had yet, forgiving him the poor skill he showed in their game of chess. Perhaps, accustomed until now to his own company, his playfellow was beginning to accept him.

He gasped as a hand clamped his throat. A violent blow hit his side so that he fell, striking the back of his head on the floor. Shadows danced in the ceiling corners of the chamber, below which a figure in dark blue doublet and hose towered over him, from this foreshortened angle looking impossibly tall. In his hands he held a footstool, poised just above John's head.

'Think you I won't drop it?' said Thomas. 'Because my father loves you? He cannot prevent accidents.'

'Thomas—' John got no further. His voice rasped in his throat.

The stool curved backwards through the air, away from its target, and fell on the bed. Pain blazed through the muscles in John's upper arms as Thomas knelt on them before letting his full weight fall on John's chest. John kicked out, gasping for air.

'*Master* Thomas to *you*!' Thomas's face bent down so close it made John's eyes ache. 'I care not that my father desires we should be brothers. I'll be no brother to a lowborn, whey-faced, scarlet-haired cur such as you! And you'll do well to remember these rules if we are to live together.'

He sat back upright, allowing John to seize his breath, and smiled down at him. 'First, you lie not on the bed until I give you leave. Second, it is for you to put all in order in the chamber each morning, that my father may be pleased when he inspects, and third' – the smile grew wider as Thomas put his head on one side – 'marking how well you acquitted yourself in our Latin hours today, each night you may do my preparation before you take your rest.'

'But Thom— *Master.* Thomas. I have. My own. Preparation.' The words came out with difficulty until at last the weight on John's chest lightened, freeing his lungs to take great gulps of air.

'Then you had best begin straightaway.' Rising to his feet, Thomas gestured at the table on which the candle stood. With a yawn he set himself to undoing the points of his doublet.

John rolled over on his side. Rubbing his upper arms, he dragged himself upright and staggered to the table. By heaven, he was weary. There lay his fair new copy of Lily's *Latin Grammar* and beside it, his playfellow's, each with a separate section of translation to be prepared.

His *playfellow.* That Thomas was not! He glanced at the bed. Thomas's dark head lay motionless on the pillow, the coverlet tucked fully round his sleeping form. A cold night for himself, then. And a long one.

Yet he'd gained something. Creeping to the chest at the foot of the bed, he lifted the lid. From under his linen he drew forth his most precious possession, the soft vellum notebook his master had given him but one day since.

CHAPTER FIFTEEN

Off the Hook

How evil can you get?

Henry leaned back in his chair and gazed out of the window. Light was fading. Beyond the small patch of grass, grey outlines of brambles and elder tangled together. From the shed in the corner of the garden a loose piece of felt roofing flapped in the wind.

This could be him. Slumped over a book by candlelight, struggling with French verbs or Latin poetry while Ralph snored in his comfortable bed – take away the fancy clothes, primitive lighting and bizarre sleeping arrangements and all other differences between him and John melted away.

Luckily, not quite all. *He* didn't have to worry about pleasing Ralph's dad, or losing his chance of a decent education (did they have a word for geek in Elizabethan times?). Now the whole business of Dr Northwell's book was sorted, Ralph had nothing more to threaten him with.

Closing the diary, he slipped it under the pile of comics.

On Monday he'd tell Ralph exactly where to get off.

★

'What's this?' Ralph stopped stuffing his maths book into his bag. He glanced first at Henry's hands, then his face.

Henry cleared his throat. 'Your mobile. And charger. Thanks, but I'm giving them back.'

Ralph didn't reach out to take them. His gaze flitted over Henry's shoulder and round the empty classroom. 'That's why you wanted to see me?'

Putting the phone down on Ralph's desk, Henry stepped back. 'I've returned the book too. I – I'm not doing your essay for you, Ralph.'

There. He'd said it. His bag and anorak were ready and the classroom door lay open.

Ralph picked up the mobile and charger and tossed them on top of his books. 'Right.' He nodded. 'If that's the way you want it.' Closing the bag, he swung it across his shoulder. 'You're taking quite a risk.'

Henry's stomach tightened. He'd steeled himself for anger and threats; this measured calm felt more dangerous. 'I – I'm not,' he said. 'I told you, the book's back. You can't brand me a thief, and anyway—'

'Really? On the right shelf, is it?'

Henry stiffened. He'd put it back; that was all that mattered. Hovering outside the library during the lunch hour, he'd seized the moment when Mr Johnson, the top of his head shining above its fringe of straggly hair, had swept in to ask for something from the props cupboard. While Mrs D'Arcy resisted with all her usual ferocity, he'd followed and thrust *The History of Northwell School* on to the darkest shelf he could manage. Not up in the gallery.

'I thought not,' said Ralph. 'Looks like you're going to have some explaining to do when the head finds out.'

'No!' He couldn't stop himself. '*You've* got something to explain to me! There were other copies of the book – ones we could use – and you didn't tell me!'

'Didn't ask, did you, Hamface?' Ralph strolled to the door. Turning, he said, 'I suppose you think this is over now, eh? Book back, phone back, sorted. You, squeaky clean; me, out of the picture.' He loomed forwards. 'Think again, Hamface.'

The door slammed shut behind him.

Henry let out a long breath. His shoulders ached. Letting them drop, he picked up his things from his desk.

'You OK?' The door opened again and Charlie entered, stretching his hand towards the hooks along the wall. 'Forgot my anorak.'

'Yeah. Fine.' Henry swallowed. 'I – I gave back the phone.'

Half out of the classroom, Charlie stopped. 'Ralph's phone? Why?'

Henry stared down at the floor, clutching his school bag so hard that the zip pressed into the palm of his hand. It had taken all his courage to face up to Ralph; somehow this was worse. 'I – didn't want it. He –

Ralph…' he licked his lips. 'It – it looks like we're not such good friends after all.'

Charlie came back in to the classroom and closed the door. 'Look, Henry,' he said, 'it isn't Ralph's fault you're not in the team. I mean, he may have some idea of the best players but in the end it's Mr Salt who decides.'

Henry gaped. What on earth was Charlie talking about? The team – oh yes, the football team, finalised last week; by which time all he'd felt was overwhelming relief that his name *wasn't* on the list, that there'd be two afternoons a week he could be free from Ralph's watchful eye! He gulped down a crazy urge to laugh.

Charlie looked at him more closely. 'Not the team, then.' Dropping anorak and school bag on the floor, he hoisted himself into a sitting position on a desk. 'So – what, then? Ralph was pretty angry. Nearly flattened me in the corridor just now.'

Henry hesitated. Did he have to own up to the complete idiot he'd been? Watching Charlie's feet in their scuffed shoes swing to and fro, he said, 'He – he wanted me to do something.'

'What?' Charlie's feet stopped swinging.

No help for it. Henry blurted out the whole story, unable – as usual – to stop the colour flooding his cheeks. *OK Charlie, you can let rip*, he thought as he finished.

From the desk somewhere above his gaze came a long, low whistle. 'The slimy beggar,' murmured Charlie. 'I knew he was up to something. It *was* weird, him being all over you suddenly. I mean, Ralph's a great football player and all that but he's never been particularly generous. Not unless he wants something in return. Henry, you *are* stupid—'

Henry winced. 'I know.'

'– not to have told me!' Jumping off the desk, Charlie punched him on the shoulder. 'I'd have got him off your back. Put the book in his desk and let him explain how it got there!' He picked up his bag and anorak. 'Next time, eh?'

Henry felt his face widen into a grin. 'Which there won't be!' he cried. 'Thanks, Charlie.'

''S'ok. Anyway, it's over now. You showed him.'

Yeah, he'd showed him. Ralph could threaten all he liked. But there was nothing he could do.

CHAPTER SIXTEEN

The Letter

Rachel opened the door. She stared at him, large-eyed, her mouth clamped shut. That alone meant trouble. Even without the voices breaking through from the kitchen at the end of the passage.

'– because it's in your contract.' His mum sounded weary, as if going round the same thing over and over again. 'Full pay for the first six months, then half—'

A chair scraped across the floor. An exclamation from Dad and then Mum trying again. 'Which is why they want you to come in. See if there's something else you can do, that doesn't involve heavy lift—'

Henry hunched his shoulders for the roar. It came, with the thump of a fist on the table and the rattling of mugs. 'I'm not fit for anything else, you know that! I'm a porter, that's what I do!'

A small hand seized Henry's. Through ribs pressed against his side he could feel his sister's heart beating. Kicking off his shoes, he said, 'Come on, Rach, let's go upstairs. You can show me your Barbie dolls.'

The narrow room was a tip. Dropping his bag and

anorak on the landing outside, Henry sank on to the bed. A gorilla and a giant pink rabbit fell off the end and bounced off a mauve plastic playhouse on the floor, before rolling to rest on a pile of clothes. Under the window, Rachel rummaged through a large blue toy box, from which a jumble of skinny limbs and blonde clouds of hair stuck out. Felt pens, pieces of paper and half-played board games lay strewn across the carpet between them.

'Messy girl.' Henry removed the *Dangermouse* DVD pressing into him and dropped it on the floor. It might've made the perfect Christmas present – twenty pence at St Dunstan's Primary School fete – still not the most comfortable thing to sit on.

Swivelling round, Rachel plonked an armful of dolls in a heap at his feet. Tucking her hair behind her ears, she set to work.

'I suppose it was a letter,' said Henry.

'Yup.' She adjusted the yellow and black spotted tunic over the shoulder of Stone-age Barbie before making her do the splits. 'From ockyou – ockyou – '

'Occupational Health.' Henry nodded. 'From the hospital.'

'They want Dad to do a cessment.' She moved her head from side to side, smoothing down the froth of a wedding dress on another doll. Suddenly her hands were still. 'Is that bad?'

'An assessment? Doesn't have to be.'

'Then why is Dad so—'

'Because he thinks they'll make him do a different job. Because of his back.'

He could have bitten his tongue. The head before him drooped. Bride Barbie rolled on to the floor and lay there, dress spiked upwards, one arm clamped to her ear. From somewhere below her mass of hair came Rachel's voice. 'Is – is it my fault?'

''Course not!' Henry jumped forward. 'That day he pushed you on your bike – he'd already hurt his back, remember? Moving that heavy patient and the trolley sliding away – he should've stopped and rested then, instead of ignoring it. But you know Dad.'

Rachel nodded slowly, still not looking up. A third Barbie appeared, dressed for clubbing in an off-the shoulder black top and a sparkly mini-skirt. 'So why doesn't he want to do a different job?'

The question he dreaded. Shrugging, he said, 'I – I don't know.'

'P'raps he's just got to get used to it? Like starting a new school?'

'Yes, that's it,' Henry nodded. 'Something like that.'

Something like that.

CHAPTER SEVENTEEN

The Blessings of Family Life

Walton Hall, January 1586

''Tis John, 'tis John!' Two small figures pushed past Hannah, holding the door open, and seized him, one by the right arm, the other by the folds of his hose. Laughing, John let himself be drawn down the narrow passage and into the parlour.

Oh, it was good to be with them all again! His mother putting aside her needlework and rising to embrace him, while he sought to disentangle himself from Esther and Katherine's grasp, and yet not push them away. Finally he sat down on the bench near the fire, one either side of him.

'John' – Katherine tugged at his doublet – 'John, why would you not sit with us in church today?'

A pang went through him. 'I would gladly but—'

'Katherine, you are a simpleton!' Esther leaned across him. 'I told you he must sit at the front with Sir Richard and Master Thomas, for he is of their household now.'

His younger sister's eyes glistened. 'Always, John? For ever and ever?'

A rawness rose in his throat. This would not do! And his father soon to enter from making his round of the stables, as he liked to do when he had leisure – John blinked hard. 'As to that, I don't know – but come, I have leave to spend this time between afternoon prayer and supper each Sunday with you. Is that not excellent?'

Katherine nodded. Under her coif her soft blonde curls rubbed against his side.

'And how does Master Thomas, John?' Putting down her needlework, his mother looked at him closely. 'Are you become good playfellows?'

John's gaze fell to his mother's hands, folded now on her lap. 'Master Thomas does well enough,' he replied. Would she notice that he had answered one question and not the other? He shifted in his seat, his feet sliding across the rushes on the floor.

But of course, the steady green eyes could miss nothing. 'It is hard for a child, however well-born, never to know his mother,' she said. 'Remember, but for his father, Thomas is quite alone.'

True enough. Fever had snatched away his mother and newborn brother before Thomas was three years old. A picture rose in his mind of a solitary, dark-haired little boy standing in the long gallery, looking out at rolling park land and a wide, empty sky. A lonely life indeed.

Then he remembered. 'But it wasn't always so.

Thomas told me his grandmother used to live with them.'

'Lady Greville.' A strange look flitted across his mother's face. Turning aside, she picked up her embroidery. 'She came because Sir Richard...' she stopped. Unwinding some silk from a spool, she moistened the tip to a point.

'Because?' John prompted.

The fine fingers were engaged in threading the needle. 'You must understand, John,' his mother continued after a moment, 'that Lady Alicia's death hit Sir Richard very hard. For weeks he would see nobody – not his steward, his family, his own son even. He locked himself away in the library with his books, sometimes all night long. Some say his longing to see Lady Alicia again grew so great that he even' – she broke off, as if aware suddenly of the three pairs of eyes looking at her.

That he even – what? thought John. *Wished to join his dead wife, perhaps? Poor Sir Richard!*

'I think,' continued his mother, 'if truth be told, the master was for a while not wholly in his right mind. Seeing the state of things, Lady Greville moved in, took charge of Master Thomas and set the household to rights. By and by, God be thanked, Sir Richard recovered and, I believe, was glad enough of my Lady's role in the household not to wish to change it.'

John bent forward. 'Yet it did change. Do you know why she left? It was sudden, according to Thomas, but he wouldn't talk about it.'

A faint line creased his mother's brow. 'It seems that Sir Richard and she had a falling out. My lady had succeeded in obtaining a position for him in the Queen's household, firmly believing...' she paused, pursing her lips as if considering the best way to frame what she had to say.

John waited. Beside him he felt Katherine wriggle, missing his attention, while Esther sat still, hands in her lap.

'...that both Sir Richard's and Master Thomas's fortunes,' his mother continued, 'would be advanced by their removal to Whitehall. When Sir Richard refused, preferring – as those near the master know well – the peace of the country to the intrigues of life at court, her ladyship took it ill and left.'

John gasped. 'Just like that? She abandoned her grandson over one disagreement with his father?' Alas for Thomas – to lose first his mother, now his grandmother!

His mother looked him in the eye. 'Mend your speech, John. It is not for you to talk about your betters in that way. I only tell you that you might not be too hard on your playfellow. He has not the blessings you have.' Her glance fell on his sisters as she returned to her sewing.

Sharp fingers dug into John's leg through the thickness of his hose. 'My mother means us!' hissed Esther into his ear. 'We are blessings!'

'Blessings, blessings!' Leaning two fists on his right

knee, Katherine slid off the bench and jumped up and down, the skirts of her gown flouncing around her ankles.

'Rascals, more like!' cried John, laughing. Oh, that was good too! When did he ever laugh with Thomas like this?

'That they are.'

He sprang to his feet. At the door stood his father, shoulders braced for Hannah to remove his dripping cloak and hat and whisk them to the kitchen to be dried.

'Rascals glad to welcome their brother, I see. As I am, John.' His father's expression softened and his mouth moved slightly; the closest he ever got to a smile.

★

Six weeks later John sat up straight in the darkness, screwing his eyes shut. With the *Cosmographia of Sebastian Munster* heavy on his lap, his candle guttering nearby, this was no easy matter; one false move and the whole library could catch fire. Yet it was the only way he could think of to call up that image again, the one of a sad and lonely Thomas his mother had given him that day.

It wouldn't come. His head ached with effort. Opening his eyes, he fixed them on the treasure before him. He must just not think of his foster-brother. Perhaps if his mind could lose itself instead in these marvellous maps of different lands, it might also lose the memory – all too fresh – of thumbs pressing into his throat, of a mouth so close to his ear he could feel how the words it spat twisted it out of shape: *Think you I will stand by while you steal my father's love? Cheat me of my birthright, as Jacob cheated Esau in the tapestry you admire so much?*

The pages slipped from his fingers. His hands felt hot; snatching them away, he rubbed them on his doublet. A fine return for his master's goodness, if he were to leave marks on his books! His master, who had let him handle the armillary sphere as he explained its workings, slowly at first, gathering speed as he warmed to the subject he loved, his eyes lighting up as he named each part of the strange globe of interlocking metal bands – *see, John, the little ball suspended in the centre, that is the Earth. The great ring surrounding the globe, at an angle from the vertical, that is the path of the sun, on which are marked all the constellations. The other, smaller rings are the paths of the planets.* And the pain that tightened his master's cheek when Thomas, wandering in, spied his father and his playfellow closeted together and hurled his bitter accusations!

It was no use. The pictures in his mind were too powerful. Closing the *Cosmographia*, he blew out the candle and, pushing the book before him, climbed out. The hour for recreation must be almost past: it wouldn't do for Thomas, sticky with marchpane from the kitchen, to discover how John hid himself.

CHAPTER EIGHTEEN

What Lies Hidden

Clasping his hands behind his head, Henry stretched.

From the front room below rose a deep murmur and excited giggle, accompanied by zippy music and squeaky voices blaring into life. Good. If Dad and Rachel were settling down to watch cartoons together, the row was over. For now.

Raindrops spattered the window, blotting and distorting the orange glow from the city. Reaching forwards, he closed the curtains.

So where was John hiding? In the library, that was clear; most likely in one of the gallery recesses. But to describe it as *"this dark confin'd space where I rejoice Thomas can never finde me…"*: that was pushing it, surely? All Thomas had to do was climb the staircase and look. Perhaps John counted on his tormentor's reluctance to enter the library at all.

And this was the embittered foster-son said to have cursed Walton Hall! This boy who so loved his kind master that he put up with being bullied and beaten by the master's son, his so-called playfellow – how could he have wished evil on the place? And why, when all these valuable books and weird instruments clearly excited him far more than they did his foster-brother, would he want them all to go up in smoke? Maybe years of Thomas's hostility finally drove him to revenge. Maybe.

Grasping the diary, he flicked forward a few pages. "*Friday, thise 21st daye of March*". Ah, this looked interesting.

> "*These two days Thomas hath treated me with such Courtesie it is a Marvel to all who behold it, to the no small Delighte of his Father, who holdeth that the Violence of Thomases Passion was as the Poison erupting from a Wound which now voided, is as good as heal'd.*"

Hmm. Perhaps. Strange how the word "*Poison*" seemed to linger in the air.

> "*Yet I would I could so easy banishe the Doubt from my Heart. My Companion no longer looketh upon me with Rage in his Eye. But he looketh on me oft and with a kind of Thoughtfullness.*"

A chill crept over Henry's shoulders. Rising, he went to the radiator by the door and let the heat spread through his limbs.

'Telephone, Henry!'

He sprang away from the radiator. *Telephone?* Nobody phoned him. Sometimes Charlie, needing to know what was for homework, but he'd have to be pretty desperate to survive the "Who? What? You'll see him at school tomorrow, won't you?" routine from Dad.

Halfway down the stairs, he stretched his arm over the banisters.

'Your friend Ralph.'

'*Ralph*?'

'Can't wait, apparently.' Rolling his eyes, Dad went back into the living room, closing the door behind him.

'Hallo, Hamface,' said Ralph into his ear. 'Nice talking to your dad.'

Henry gripped the handrail. It felt smooth and slippery.

'Must be really cool for you that he's around,' Ralph went on. 'Not going back to work anytime soon, is he?'

Somehow Henry made it back to the bedroom. Closing the door, he leaned back, feeling the solid wood against his shoulders. 'Ralph, what – why are you—'

'Thought you'd like to know I've solved your mystery. I'm quite pleased with myself.'

'Wh-what mystery?'

'Want me to spell it out? Hey, that's quite funny. *Spell* it – like words. Get it?'

No. Not this.

'It all made sense. You reading your dad the Sunday newspaper, the look of terror on your face if anyone comes to your house, your dad mistaking bicarb for baking powder or whatever because they'd changed the colour of the packaging – it all added up.'

The room spun. Pain throbbed in his ear, pressed

against the receiver. He forced his arm to relax but now he couldn't hold the phone still, his whole body shook. 'R-Ralph, pl-please—'

'There I was, thinking aaah, what a nice, cosy scene, father and son together…' Ralph paused, as if savouring the picture. 'And it's all because your dad needs you to read to him! *He can't read!*'

'No! Please, Ralph, no!' Oh great, he was sobbing – how pathetic was that? And pleading with Ralph, of all people!

Laughter sliced down the telephone. '*That's* why he can't go back to work. His back's shot and he doesn't want anyone to know he's got the reading level of a five-year-old! Or less!'

'Shut up, shut UP!'

'With pleasure.' Ralph stopped laughing. 'I can shut up if you like. I understand why you keep it secret. I mean, my dad can be a right jerk; but at least I don't have to be ashamed of him.'

Henry clenched his fist. In his mind he smacked it hard into that jeering, triumphant face, knuckles cracking on bone, blood bursting through flesh…

'So don't worry,' Ralph continued. 'I won't tell anyone. If you see sense, that is.'

See sense. At that moment Henry saw nothing. The colour behind his eyelids changed from pink to black as he shut them so tight nothing could escape. No tears. He couldn't speak. Not a sound came from his throat but his narrow, trapped breathing.

'Good,' said Ralph. 'Two weeks till the essay deadline. That should be plenty.'

The line went silent. For a moment Henry stayed where he was, phone pressed to his ear, fingernails digging into his cheek.

Dropping his arm, he stumbled out on to the landing. Clouds of steam billowing from the kitchen below told him supper was nearly ready, spaghetti by the look of it; and – from the sweet, savoury aroma – accompanied by bacon and tomato sauce, a combination usually designed to make his mouth water. Not today. Not with this wave of nausea rising inside him. One hand on the banister rail, he slowly descended the stairs.

Strange noises came from the front room. The squeak and chatter of TV cartoons had given way to rustlings, murmurings and the occasional bump. Pushing open the door, Henry felt something resisting him. He peered round.

'Shush.' Curled up on the floor, Rachel grinned and put a finger to her lips.

Beyond her, near the television, stood Dad, his eyes hidden under a length of navy blue and yellow Henry recognised as his school scarf. 'Hmm, now where is that rascally Rachel?' he said. 'Must be around here somewhere.' His large hand ran across the screen, through the air and hit the standard lamp in the corner by the window. Already wonky, the shade slipped, exposing the light bulb. 'Aha!' He seized the wooden stem. 'Here we are.'

Rachel snorted. 'Silly! I'm not a lamp!'

'What's that?' Dad stood up straight. 'Did someone speak?'

Slipping past the sofa, Henry replaced the phone in its holder on the side table. Rachel managing to persuade Dad to play her favourite game of Blind Man's Buff was a good sign. He must have got over the letter, or – more likely – was trying to. And at least someone was having fun round here.

Going into the kitchen, he watched his mum heap spaghetti on to four plates and knew he could eat none of it.

'Are you all right, Henry?' Mum stopped mid-scoop. 'You look very pale. I hope you're not overworking, up there in your room all the time.'

'Not work, though, is it?' Dad patted Henry's shoulder as he and Rachel squeezed past him to take their seats. 'Not when it's for the essay prize.'

Henry sat down and took a deep breath. 'Thing is Dad, I – well – I've changed my mind. I – don't think I'll enter after all.'

'What?' Dad put down his forkful. 'What's this?'

Mum turned and looked at him. Even Rachel paused in her chewing, mouth bulging, to glance first at Mum and Dad, then straight at Henry.

Now he was for it. Tucking his hands underneath him to stop them shaking, Henry shrugged his shoulders, as if he didn't care all that much. 'I just don't want to do it, that's all. It is a lot of extra work.'

Returning the empty pan to the cooker, Mum sat down slowly. 'But – but you've done so much already,' she said. 'All that time in the town library – and you found it really interesting.'

'Not *that* interesting.' Henry stuck out his bottom lip. 'And I probably won't win, so what's the point?'

Dad banged his hand on the table. 'I'll tell you what the point is, Henry. You won't win if you don't try! If you don't succeed, fine, but at least you'll have given it a go. Failure comes from not trying at all!' Stabbing his fork on to his plate, he drove it ferociously through the spaghetti.

Henry's heart seemed to swell in his chest. 'No, Dad, it's not that! It's…' he stopped. 'I just – just…' What could he say? 'The others – they're so clever. Much cleverer than me.' He cringed. How lame could he be?

It worked. The look in his dad's eyes softened. 'So that's it.' Reaching out, he found Henry's right hand and gave it a squeeze. 'They're not, you know. They may act like it but— '

'No one'f cleverer than you, Henry!' cried Rachel, scattering tomato droplets all around.

'– you won the scholarship, don't forget. You've got as much chance as any of them. More, probably. Now' – he gave Henry's hand a final pat – 'eat up. You'll feel better with something inside you.'

Tiredness swept over Henry. He couldn't fight this anymore, not right now. Picking up his fork, he wound it into the spaghetti, watching the glistening, slippery strands glide through the tines.

He must just stop thinking about it. Put it out of his mind, at least for now. Eat a few mouthfuls – enough to satisfy his mum's watchful eye – then make his escape. If only he could lose himself in something, just like John Striven did, poring over those ancient books in the library to banish Thomas from his thoughts!

John Striven… a shape rose up in Henry's mind. A soft, cream-coloured book with thick pages covered in faded brown writing. It must still be lying open on his desk where he left it.

CHAPTER NINETEEN

Deep Water

Walton Hall, July 1586

There had been no rain for weeks. Heat hovered above the paths in the herb garden, where the flagstones gave back the warmth poured into them since early morning. John blinked. Even now, in this blessed hour of recreation after supper, the flash of glass from the windows of the north-east wing and tower dazzled him.

'Quick, John!' Ahead, Thomas ran through the low gate that led out into the yard.

There too, the ground was dry as dust, heat beating out from the brick walls of the brew house and dairy. The hens, forsaking their scratching on the cobbles, lay still, limp-feathered, in what shade they could find. John's legs in their thick stockings chafed as he quickened his pace past the stables to the road leading out of the yard, where at last a breeze lifted the hair from his neck. To the east, waves of yellowing grass rolled away to a brightness that made him shade his eyes: the cool, beckoning river, with the hay meadow on the far side and beyond, the blue hills fading into sky.

Twenty paces on Thomas bounded over the ground, his black hair glinting in the sun. At the oak tree he stopped and nudged with his foot a soft, golden shape lying stretched out and panting in the shade. 'Get up, Flash, you idle bitch.'

The spaniel lifted her head and looked imploringly first at him, then at John drawing near.

'Leave her, Thomas, it's too hot,' said John. 'Let them all rest.' Beside Flash lay two half-grown puppies, their young fur pale and curling on their long droopy ears and splayed paws.

'So? She might cool herself with us in the river,' said Thomas. Shrugging, he started off again, though more slowly now, his cheeks glowing, a bead of sweat on his brow. Ahead the water sparkled.

John followed. Close to, the river looked wider. Overhanging banks cast deep shadows; here and there blades of grass and twigs floated swiftly over the dark surface. In the back of John's mind something stirred.

'Frightened by a drop of water?' challenged Thomas. His doublet undone, he drew it off, not troubling to undo the points that attached it to his hose but peeling all off as one garment. Kicking it away, he pulled at his stockings. His shoes he had already discarded.

John began tugging at the neck of his doublet to undo it, his fingers clumsy with sweat. 'You can swim,' he mumbled. 'I can't.'

Thomas flashed him a smile. 'We will but cool our legs,' he said. 'Have no fear.' He sprang into the water, shirt flapping. 'Come, it is delicious!' His eyes were black slits.

Water droplets fell on John's hand, sending a shiver through his hot skin. In a moment he pulled off his outer clothes, shirt billowing round his legs. The shock of cold water, a gasp, and his feet sank into the soft river bed. A splash hit his face; through shimmering vision he saw Thomas grin and break the surface again with his foot before plunging away down the shallows. Huzzah! John threw himself after, splashing and laughing, stirring up great clouds of mud, shaking off the tendrils that curled softly round his ankles.

The tendrils… In deeper water, weeds grew longer. The current flowed swiftly above his knees. Looking at the bank, four, no, five yards away, he felt his stomach lurch. How had that distance grown so quickly? Pulling hard, he aimed for where Thomas was heaving himself out of the water to sit on the edge – and staggered back. It was deeper there, not shallower; up to his thighs at least, and the weeds thicker and stronger.

A breeze rustled along the black surface. 'Thomas' – John's voice wouldn't keep steady – 'I don't know how to come to you. Show me.'

His playfellow pointed downstream. 'That way! The shallows lie there.'

No shallows. John's foot trod nothing. As his mouth opened to cry out, water poured in and down his throat.

He lunged with his arms and legs, meeting only weeds trailing through emptiness, while there, beyond the surface breaking into his eyes, the grass-topped bank danced out of reach.

Empty. No sign of Thomas.

★

Henry's head shot back, hitting the wall above his bed. For a moment everything around him revolved slowly as he waited for the pain to subside and his heart to stop pounding. On the bedside table the hands of his alarm clock pointed to 12.15 am.

No. It was late, he should be asleep, how would he wake in the morning? But he couldn't stop now. OK, so maybe reading page after page of John Striven's diary wasn't the best way to take his mind off his own problems. Not when all it did was to show him another Ralph in another age!

Yet this one was worse. A murderer.

The word sent shockwaves through his body. But it was true! Just because Thomas didn't – couldn't have – succeeded, did that make him any less guilty? Luring his foster-brother into deep water, knowing he'd drown, which he would have if – if…

He looked again at the last few lines of the entry for *"Saturday, thise 12th of July 1586"*.

"By God's Grace I did not drowne, for that noble dog

Flash alerted by my crie with much Barking brought men to my aide and indeed would have drawn me out herself, had her Strengthe allowed her. Thomas now does sweare it was hee rais'd the alarm and I wish it were so but how can I be sure? Rather I fear that Thomas is set on finding a way to kill me, whereby no Suspicion will fall on him. I know not what to do. For how will I be believ'd? Not by my Master, for whom such Wickednesse in his own Sone is not to be thought of. Nor by my Father, who will take it for Malice on my part and be asham'd of me. Yet if I cannot speke, I must find a means to Protect myself."

This was unbearable. So it wasn't enough for John to survive one "accident": he had to go on living with this psychopath – sleeping in the same bed as him, even – with no one to believe his story!

Leaning back, Henry closed his eyes. Being blackmailed by Ralph was bad but at least he wasn't trying to kill him. John Striven's tormentor was in a completely different league. Maybe their situations weren't so alike after all.

And yet…

A means to protect myself. The words swirled in his mind, like weeds trailing through black water. Softness spread through his limbs. There was something he wanted to know, some answer to a question not yet formed… and as he sank into darkness the answer came.

Yes, I found it. Stronger than you can imagine.

CHAPTER TWENTY

A Rediscovery

Walton Hall, July 1586

Closing the library door, John gave a swift glance round before advancing down the room. He should be safe enough. Sir Richard and his steward had ridden out early in the morning to see how the haymaking progressed and would be away all day.

Reaching the right-hand staircase, he turned to the wall under the gallery. Here, among the oldest books, many shelved with their spines pointing inwards in the old style, was the likeliest resting place for the manuscript Sir Richard removed from the lectern that first day. John had never thought to look for it before; but nor had he been in such dire need as he was now.

After a couple of false tries, his fingers closed on a thickly-folded wedge of parchment. As he pulled it out the fold sprang open, almost as if the manuscript longed to be freed from its confinement and share its secrets once more. A thrill darted through him as he recognised the strange assortment of images: the sun, shooting flames, the crescent moon, the woman with the long, golden hair; and in the centre, the robed man pointing a sword whose tip outlined a circle containing a five-point star. *"The menes by whiche the Naturall Philosopher may Summon an Angellick Spirit to assiste him in Grete Perplexitie…"* An angel, that was what he needed! A heavenly being to defend him from any more murderous attempts by Thomas! True, John was no natural philosopher, not yet, but did that matter? He was in great perplexity, that was certain. Taking a few seconds to memorise the diagram with its Latin incantation written underneath, he closed the manuscript – only for a piece of paper to fall from between the folds and flutter to the floor.

He picked it up. It was a letter; or rather, a part of one, since the top line began halfway through a sentence:

"…well understand but cannot agree with your Caution in this matter. Because some Demons may prove to be Evill it followeth not that there are none that are Good. Whoever striveth to unlock the Secrets of Nature, thus revealing the Power and Greatness of the Creator, may ask in all humilitie for assistance from any one of the thousands of Spirits dwellinge betweene heaven and earth. That great man of God and philosophie, Trithemius, sheweth thise in his Wondrous Worke Steganographia, *in which he listeth all the names of Angells and how each is to be address'd; indeed I have it on good authoritie that he himself did summon the Spirit of a great lady back from the dead for*

the comfort of her grieving husband. In light of your late
sad loss I praye this knowledge may be of use to you.
Your assur'd friend
John Dee
Mortlake, this 5th of November 1576"

The letter trembled in John's hand. Clamping it between the parchment folds, he pushed the manuscript back into the shelf and stood for a moment, breathing hard.

The manuscript. Had Sir Richard obtained it, not just to read, but to *make use of*? A memory flashed through John's mind. His mother sewing by candlelight, a sentence begun and broken off: *Such was Sir Richard's longing to see Lady Alicia again that he even…* Was *that* the rumour behind her words? In his own moment of greatest need Sir Richard hadn't, as John thought, wished to join his wife; but rather *to call her spirit back from the dead?*

Dizziness seized him. Clutching the bookshelf he grappled with the thoughts and questions shooting through his brain. Did his master do it? Did that account for the long hours – whole nights even – he spent locked in the library after Lady Alicia's death? If so – and now another feeling surged through John, sweeping all weakness away – if Sir Richard, overcoming his doubts, appealed for angelic assistance, then so could he!

John strode back down the library. He must give

Thomas no inkling of his plan. The picture stood fresh in his mind, as did the charm bordering it, calling on spirits of earth, air, fire and water; he'd transfer all to his diary later.

Then, as soon as a moment presented itself, to work.

CHAPTER TWENTY-ONE

Summoning Aid

So what did he do?

The question ran round and round Henry's mind like a hamster on a wheel. Obviously John found a solution. How else could he have survived, living close to a foster-brother capable of staging any number of "accidents"? The diary went on until December 1586; even finishing then didn't mean anything. Sir Richard probably gave him a new notebook every year. And whatever means he used to keep Thomas at bay – well, couldn't that also work for someone who didn't want to kill you as such, just wreck your life?

Smack. Henry nearly fell off his chair. A thin book with a laminated cover lay quivering on his desk. Large black letters framed the portrait of a balding man with a ruff around his neck, a high forehead and strong dark eyes.

'It's *Romeo and Juliet*, not a chunk of the Rosetta Stone,' said Mr Johnson from somewhere above his head. 'Act Three, Scene One. To read in class today; learn some for homework tonight. Do wake up, Henry.'

Henry didn't move. Mr Johnson, battered tweed jacket trailing a whiff of mothballs, continued round the class amidst a ripple of laughter. It didn't matter. All that mattered was not to look up and meet Ralph's cool, triumphant gaze trained on him from the other side of the room. Or – worse, almost – Charlie's bewildered expression as he tried to catch his eye, as he'd been trying to do all morning. *Something's wrong,* it said. *So why won't you tell me? Like we agreed?*

How long could he last this out? Science and maths had passed in a daze. No relief even during lunch break when Charlie, thinking to cheer him up, challenged him to a game in which he lost two (two!) giant squids because how could he aim straight with *him* watching his every move? Worse, it looked as if it was Meena who'd put him off, since for some reason she'd taken to dawdling past as they played their games.

One more lesson to go; then home, as fast as possible, and see if there was anything in John Striven's diary, anything at all that could help him. That way he could deal with Ralph and there'd be no need to bother Charlie because… because… well, why not? If he could confide in anyone, it was Charlie.

Straightaway his dad's face rose before him, lines creasing his forehead and a troubled look in his eyes. *You'd do that, son? Tell a school mate about me?*

A sick feeling rose in his stomach. *No, Dad, it's OK.*

He wouldn't be bothering Charlie.

★

Three hours later, Henry sat at his desk at home, reading the entry for *"Friday, thise 18th July"* for the third time. Clearly he hadn't quite mastered this Elizabethan writing; because John couldn't have written what Henry thought he had.

He turned the page. There, before him, lay John's version of the drawing he'd just described with such eagerness, the same strange words scrawled alongside: *"terrae aerii ignei aquatani spiritus, salvete"*. Henry stared at it until his eyes hurt.

This was John's solution? He used a *spell* to protect himself from his enemy? He couldn't have. Or he could – from what Dr Northwell wrote he had plenty of magical books to choose from – but it was all nonsense, surely.

Unless…

Unless it was enough just to believe he wasn't on his own. That something – or someone – was giving him supernatural power. The question was: did it work? Henry's eye ran down the page, stopping at *"Monday, thise 21st day of July"*:

"Alle is so different in my Life I know not where to begynn, save to thank from the bottom of my Heart this Kind Spirit, this Mephistopheles, who answer'd my anguish'd call. Indeed so swiftly did he appear and look'd about him with such Joy that it was as if he knew his way and but

awaited my Summons. Though in outline more corporeal than I imagin'd a Creature of Air to be, his Blessed, Life Preservinge Gift is sure proof of his Angellick Powere; nor will he return to reclaim this Stone, whiche holdeth in its Hearte that Preciouse Liquid he dothe call Quintessence, until my Dayes draw near their Ende, for which I am right thankfull.

To give my Soule in exchange for this Bountie is no losse, since my Soule is God's already and such a Gift could not come except by His Goodnesse."

A tingling ran down Henry's spine. This was more than John psyching himself up. Relief erupted from the page, as if someone really had come to his aid. But – a *Kind Spirit*?

Henry stared at the diary until the lines of writing danced. Either John was letting his imagination run away with him or… or he'd gone crazy. This 'spirit', Mephistopheles (how do you even pronounce that?), was the product of a mind strained to breaking point by months of torment, for which the narrow escape from death had been the last straw. Wouldn't that be enough to send anyone over the edge? What if the rest of the diary just showed John losing his mind completely?

Henry turned the page.

"Thise Quintessence is beyond all Imaginings a Marvellous Gift. It taketh me little Labour or none to render the Obscurest Latin and French into English and I

am so much improv'd in castinge Accounts that Doctor Thorne is quite amaz'd. But yet of greater Note is my new Prowess in Fencing. Thomases Astonishmente when I did today score three direct Hits together gave me more Satisfaction than I can expresse. More, had I not parried well I had receiv'd some Grievous Woundes, the tip of Thomas's foil having no button, a strange circumstance for which I can well guess the cause."

Henry sucked in his cheeks. This didn't sound like the ravings of a madman. Yet if John was telling the truth, the gift he'd received was extraordinary. What kind of stone was this that could transform your skills at both sport and school work, as well as provide protection from someone out to kill you? A kind Henry would give anything for, that's what. As would everyone he knew.

He frowned, biting his lips together. There must be an explanation. This Mephistopheles... from John's own account, he sounded a pretty solid guy, nothing airy about him. Perhaps an old friend of Sir Richard's had chosen that moment to pay him a visit and, seeing the state his poor foster-son was in, decided to boost his morale. A priest even – yes! That would explain the stuff about John's soul. Handing him a beautiful stone and telling him it would protect him, give him strength – well, couldn't that be enough for it to work? Self-belief was everything, according to Dad. And he – Henry grimaced – should know.

Dad.

When he was little, it hadn't mattered. Playing football in the recreation ground, or flying a kite; clamping his fist to the hammer so Henry could bang the nails into the shed they made together; picture books, even. Only when the black squiggly lines began to make the pictures in his head did Henry look up and see his dad's solitary figure seeming to grow smaller and further away, left behind on an island to which he himself could never return.

Self-belief. What a complete con. Self-belief might have helped John Striven but it wouldn't get Ralph off his back. No way out for him. No magic stone. No sword even to try what John had done. There was only one solution.

Ralph could have the wretched essay. Then he'd be off the hook, once and for all.

CHAPTER TWENTY-TWO

The Screw Tightens

'Hey, Hamface. I get the impression you've been avoiding me.'

Henry's fingers slipped off the door handle. He almost fell back into the boys' washroom.

'No use hiding in there. Gotta come out some time.'

'I wasn't…' his voice stuck in his throat. Swallowing, he strained to see past the figure leaning with one hand against the corridor wall. Oh no, where was everybody? He must have miscalculated the end of lunch break. The dining room opposite lay empty, a distant clatter of crockery and hot smell of dishwasher wafting through from the kitchens beyond. Bare tarmac showed through the glass in the swing doors to outside: what, no one even in the playground? 'Ralph, we're late, we'd better go.'

'Yeah,' said Ralph, sticking out his other arm just as Henry tried to walk past. 'Thought you were cutting it a bit fine. 'Specially with Mr Johnson. I hope you won't be doing that with the essay deadline. Wednesday today. You've got till Monday week, OK?'

Eyes on the floor, Henry nodded.

'Good.' Dropping his arm, Ralph made for the door. 'That's all I wanted to know. Come on, then.'

Halfway across the playground Henry mustered his thoughts. 'Ralph, I'll – I'll do the essay for you. Then – that's it, right? We'll be quits.'

Ralph bent his head slightly, with the air of a patient adult indulging a child. 'Sure. Don't suppose there's anything else I'll want you to do.' Entering the classroom block, he sauntered towards the stairs.

Henry followed. His stomach felt hollow. Murmurings from behind closed doors along the corridor showed how late they were but that wasn't enough to explain the growing unease inside him. And yet the worst was over, surely? The deal was hateful but he'd accepted it. Once Ralph had his hands on the essay, he'd leave him in peace.

Shoulder to the classroom door, Ralph smiled. 'If there is, I'll let you know.'

On either side of Henry white walls soared upwards before closing in somewhere above his head. His knees gave way and he leaned against the doorframe, breathing hard. Something was odd about the classroom: figures clustered in front of him where there should have been a clear view of desks, making it easy for two latecomers to slip in – but he hardly cared. His mind was filled to bursting with Ralph's last words. *If there is…* He wasn't out of it then! He would never be out! He was safe only until Ralph wanted something else. What kind of safety was that?

'Well, I don't know why you should look so aghast at a bit of Shakespeare in action, Henry, but that's the perfect expression for Romeo. Come on, don't hang back.'

'What –?' The room slid into focus. Two figures in front moved, revealing a ring of people leaning against desks pushed back against the classroom walls.

In the open space in the centre stood Mr Johnson, holding something long and thin towards him. As Henry reached to take it, his fingers closed on cold metal, a handle nestling in his palm, protected from the thin blade by a hilt... Ah, now he remembered. The scene they read in English yesterday: today they were acting it out. Charlie, nearby, shot him a grin. He too held a sword in his hand.

A *sword*. Henry felt its weight, balancing it in his grasp. Light flashed as he swung the blade upwards, his gaze running along the length to the tip: not very sharp – it came from the theatre props cupboard, after all. But sharp enough.

'Hey, be careful,' cried Mr Johnson. 'And Romeo is holding back in this scene, remember? He's torn between the two sides, Montagues and Capulets, hence his – your – tortured expression.' A few people sniggered but Henry barely heard. 'Whereas Mercutio' – Mr Johnson nodded at Charlie – 'and Tybalt are pursuing gangland warfare – ah, we don't have a Tybalt yet.'

Hands shot up. 'Let me see...' Sweeping the circle of eager faces, Mr Johnson's eyes fell on a figure leaning back against a desk, arms folded, a smile on his lips. 'Ralph. Yes. You'll do. Now, books open, everybody, and we'll go from Romeo's entry.'

A crackle and rustle of paper. Henry didn't move. Somebody – was it Charlie? – thrust a square shape with a cool, laminated feel into his left hand. He stared down at the open page. Words broke up and faded away and all he could see was the dim outline of a figure in a long robe holding a sword and beside him, a five-point star.

'Well, peace be with you, sir. Here comes my—'

'Wait, Ralph! And Charlie – both of you, just *look at the text*.' From somewhere far away came Mr Johnson's exasperated voice. 'You don't draw yet, not by a long—'

'*What* is going on here?'

A sudden silence. Henry's mind jolted back. A tall figure in a navy blue cape stood in the doorway, surveying the scene, taking in Ralph's raised arm. In one swift movement, she crossed the floor and flicked out her hand. 'I'll take charge of that, Rafe, thank you.' The cape swirled. 'And – that one, too.'

'But—'

'Hey!'

Ralph's smooth features creased into a scowl. Charlie opened his unexpectedly free right hand in a gesture of surprise.

No. Not his. Henry tightened his grip. Keeping his eyes on the deputy head's profile, he shrank back into the crowd, sword pressing the length of his leg. The lockers weren't far away, and in the corner, an empty one.

'I see this is an exciting lesson, Mr Johnson.' From the side Mrs James's smile gave her the look of an ancient Egyptian statue. 'But allowing pupils to use real weapons is just a little *too* exciting.'

Henry's left hand touched one of the lockers. He felt his way along.

'Real weapons?' Mr Johnson gaped like a startled frog. Slack folds of skin wobbled on his neck. 'Of course they're not real. Look how short and blunt they are. If I thought they were dangerous—'

The firm smile broadened. 'Blunt or not, they have points. As such they are in breach of health and safety guidelines.'

'Mrs James,' said Mr Johnson, 'I have been teaching Shakespeare for over thirty years and there has never been so much as a *scratch*…'

Closing the locker, Henry edged back to the circle of people and glanced at the clock on the wall. Half-past two. One hour till home time. By the time someone remembered the third sword, he'd be well away.

CHAPTER TWENTY-THREE

In the Thicket

It was still dark outside. Squares of electric light in the backs of distant houses gave a smudgy glow through the early morning fog. Henry's hand, releasing the curtains, swirled on the wet glass.

He dressed quickly. Not just because time was short but to give himself something to occupy his mind. Underwear, shirt, trousers, socks – there. He was ready. Just like any school day really. Only today he happened to be going early, that was all.

That was all. Yeah, right. Who was he trying to kid? He was going to do it, that's what this was about. Summoning a spirit had worked for John Striven; why not for him too?

Reaching into the wardrobe, he pulled out the long thin shape, wrapped half in plastic, half in his sweatshirt, and slid it into his book bag. With his sweatshirt scrunched round the handle, you couldn't tell what it was: it just looked as if he'd stuffed his bag carelessly. Which was how he'd smuggled the sword home in the first place.

Opening the door, he glanced across the landing. Rachel's room was empty – if you ignored the wash of clothes, dolls, shoes, books and piles of sparkly clutter across the floor. The door to Mum and Dad's room, too, stood ajar; well, that figured. Dad was showering and Mum wasn't due back from her night shift for nearly an hour.

Gripping his school bag, he went downstairs to the kitchen. 'Rachel,' he whispered.

At the table a pyjama-clad figure knelt on a chair, hugging a large box of cereal to her chest. In the midst of pouring she looked up. A cloud of soft pale hailstones splashed over her bowl and on to the table.

'Not so much!' Henry hissed.

The box remained suspended as Rachel looked him up and down. Her eyes grew round. 'Ooh, you're already dressed!' she said. 'But it's only…' the chair wobbled as she swivelled round to look at the cooker.

'Seven-thirty, I know. Look, could you tell Mum and Dad for me? I've got to be at school early today. Got things to do.' That sounded impressive. Enough for her, anyway.

She nodded.

'Great. Bye then.'

Behind him came the crunch of the rice crispy box being put down on the table. Then, 'Are there buses this early?'

An arrow dart. Enough to check him in his stride. 'Of course,' he said. 'Lots and lots.' Grabbing his anorak from the hook, he risked a look round.

He needn't have worried. Concentrating on carrying a spoonful of sugar, none too steadily, through the air, she didn't give him a glance.

It hadn't exactly been a lie. He never said he'd be taking the bus. What use would that be, getting him to school a full hour before registration? What with the caretaker unlocking all the doors and teachers arriving with their loads of exercise books, he'd stand out a mile. Impossible to slip away somewhere and do what he wanted without being disturbed.

Pulling the front door quietly to behind him, he headed down the path and through the gate. The darkness was thinning. Street lamps shone through the billowing fog, orange patches of light etched with fine drizzle. A few cars swished past as he walked along, their headlights looming through the mist like pale ghosts. Reaching the ring road, he turned left down the cycle path that ran alongside it. Traffic was busier here, but the high hedge on his right dulled the sound, while the rough outline of hawthorn, blackthorn and brambles on his left marked where fields and water meadows spread towards Northwell School, lying just on the edge of the town centre. Spanning the gap between the nearby houses and the first ploughed field lay the recreation ground, bordered by a sandy, tree-lined track, a favourite route for dog-walkers. Not at this hour and in this weather though; with luck there'd be no one around at all.

Leaving the cycle path for the track, he walked for a

hundred metres or so to a spot where a narrow path threaded off into thick clumps of trees before widening into a clearing. Dropping the book bag, he glanced round. Above him, bare branches stood out against the whitening sky. But lower down, a tangle of brambles, elder, holly and last year's weeds gave cover enough. He stood still and listened: pigeons cooing from the branches above; traffic humming on the ring road and, somewhere in the distance, the dry rumble and crash of the rubbish collection lorry. Otherwise all was still.

Cold numbed his fingers as he unfastened his bag and pulled out the sword, unwrapping the sweatshirt from round the handle. Grasping it, he felt a quiver shoot through his body. It could've been made for him! The metal nestled in his palm, its roundness fitting the contours of his hand, the blade – about as sharp as a school canteen knife, whatever Mrs James might think – the perfect weight and length. For a moment he held it upright; then he pointed it to the ground. Closing his eyes, he spoke the words he'd carefully memorised: *'Terrae aerii ignei aquatani spiritus, salvete.'*

A delicious tingling ran through his fingers and up his arm. From somewhere deep within he felt a tremendous strength surge upwards, gather itself and focus in one long arc through his body, down his arm and along the blade. Trees, bushes, the clearing itself, all dissolved into mist. His hand swept round to describe a wide circle on the ground and then, with a lightness that astonished him, flicked back and forth to create five true, straight lines. Dropping his arm, he let a smile of triumph spread across his face. Outlined on the damp earth before him lay a perfectly drawn five-point star. He stood back, panting, and waited.

The mist faded. Brambles, thorn and holly resumed their shapes. Drops glistened on cobweb strands spun between dead weed stalks that bordered the path winding out of the clearing.

Henry's cheeks began to ache under his smile. His hand, relaxing its grip, felt stiff, pulled down by the weight of the sword that a moment ago had seemed fused to it, as if blade and arm were one. It didn't feel like that now. Dropping the sword, he rubbed his shoulder with his left hand. Nothing was going to happen. It had been a pointless, mad idea. Did he really think drawing a pretty pattern on the ground and chanting some strange words would get Ralph off his back? He jabbed his feet at the markings before him, smudging them into the earth. That did it; wiped away all evidence of his stupidity, even if he couldn't from his own mind.

Picking up the sword, he rewound the sweatshirt round the handle and slid it into his bag. A two-kilometre walk lay before him; if he hurried, he'd make it to school before 8.45 am.

A sound tore through the bushes at his back. He whirled round. It came again, unevenly, and his heart almost melted with relief. *It's only a dog barking, idiot.* Bending to pick up his bag he spotted, through a gap in the branches, a large black creature padding towards him down the track. There was something odd about its soft outline, its delicate pointed muzzle and floppy ears topped by a rounded woolly crown… a *poodle*? Who on earth owned a poodle in this neighbourhood? Let alone one as big as this. Or with eyes that – glowed like fire.

Henry's heart stood still. In his mind another pair of eyes stared at him out of the darkness of a long, book-lined gallery.

He straightened up. *Keep calm*, he told himself. *Breathe evenly. You're over all that now.* Having let his imagination run wild in the library, was he now going to be spooked by someone's pet poodle? The mist must be freezing his brain or something. He'd better get going.

Setting off down the narrow path, he glanced through gaps between trunks and clumps of brambles. The dog was still there, moving almost parallel to him. Odd that no other figure appeared, he thought. The owner must have passed by already, just at the moment he'd been making a complete fool of himself in the clearing. Well, so what if they did; they wouldn't have seen anything. The bushes were too thick for that. Hoisting his school bag on to his shoulder, Henry quickened his pace.

Six metres from the main track he stopped, his heart slamming against his ribs.

CHAPTER TWENTY-FOUR

The Kind Spirit

A man stood leaning against a beech tree in the fork between the track and the path. Hands flat against the silvery-grey trunk and eyes closed, he tilted his face eastwards, as if to catch whatever warmth he could from the sun rising somewhere behind thick cloud. His chin ended in a small, pointed beard, black as the thick curls that fell back to touch his collar… except that it wasn't a collar but, well, a ruff. White and finely creased, it framed his head in a perfect circle above a high-necked, thickly-padded velvet jacket. Instead of trousers, he wore a puffy kind of shorts over tights and high leather boots. Slashes cut into his sleeves showed glimpses of a white shirt underneath; apart from that, and scarlet stripes in his shorts, he was dressed entirely in black.

Henry stared. What was this: an actor? A *weirdo*? The path led directly to him. Henry could creep past; the guy had his eyes shut, after all. Or he could cut through the trees and make a detour. It might be wisest.

'Stay.'

Henry stood still. The voice seemed to bore through his back.

'See, I am here, at your service.'

A nutter. That was all he needed. Henry's heart beat in his throat. 'I'm all right, thanks.' He could make a run for it. Those leather over-the-knee boots looked flashy enough but hardly made for speed. He'd be OK. Unless – unless that had been *his* dog that passed earlier and he set it on Henry.

Sweat stuck the shirt to the back of Henry's neck. Out of the corner of his eye he saw the man shift his position slightly, adjusting a short, thick-pleated cloak that hung from one shoulder. A faint smile curled his thin lips. 'If that were so,' he said, 'you would not have called me.'

'*Called*?' Henry choked. 'I didn't. I – I don't know you.'

The man gave a dismissive shake of his head. From his velvet cap set at a jaunty angle, a long, iridescent blue-green feather nodded. 'Few men do, until the moment comes. It makes no difference.'

Crazy, definitely. Keep him talking, that was the thing, till he'd got safely past. 'I was watching the dog,' said Henry, 'the poodle. Is – is he yours?'

The man's smile broadened. His eyes were like two dark stones. 'In a manner of speaking.'

What was that supposed to mean? It didn't matter. He'd have to risk it. There'd be plenty of people on the cycle path by now; surely if they saw a dog going for someone in the recreation ground, they'd stop and help.

'You summoned Mephistopheles, Henry. What is your wish?'

The ground swayed. Through clouded vision he saw a black shape detach itself from the grey trunk, a flash of scarlet lining as the cloak swirled, then the man stood only a couple of paces away, examining him.

'You are in great need of something,' he said. 'Not the usual, though, by my guess.'

Henry blinked. On the far side of the beech tree, beyond the track, the recreation ground stretched away in patches of mud and thinning grass. And on this side of the tree…

Elation rushed through him. It had worked! This was *him* – John Striven's Kind Spirit – come to his aid! All he had to do was tell his story, pour everything out – but his tongue stuck to the roof of his mouth.

The man seemed untroubled by his silence. 'Power, riches, a beautiful woman?' he continued conversationally, stroking his beard. 'No. In my experience when one as young as you calls me, it is because an enemy has him by the throat.'

As Thomas had John, flashed through Henry's mind.

A gleam came into the man's eye. 'Yes, indeed,' he said. 'Young Walton.'

Henry stood rigid. How did the guy *know*? Had he spoken out loud? How, when his voice refused to obey him?

'Thomas Walton, son of Sir Richard,' the man repeated, 'whose violent inclinations caused young

Striven to seek my aid. Ah, poor fellow.' He spoke softly, but his eyes gleamed more strongly than ever, with a flicker of something like excitement in their depths. 'And you, young master? Are you in a similar plight that you copy Striven's remedy?'

He couldn't stop it. Ralph's image cut straight through his thoughts: bright, mocking, his head thrown back as if it was all easy, so easy, and so *amusing*... He nodded.

'Excellent.' The man drew himself up. In the pale light the blue-green feather danced. 'A most favourable set of circumstances. I will take care of your enemy if you, in return, will do something for me. We have a bargain.'

'A – bargain?' Somewhere inside Henry an uneasy feeling stirred.

The man smiled. 'Allay your fears. It is not your soul I want.'

His *soul*? The words struck chill. Should he be glad this Mephistopheles guy didn't want his soul? John had promised his own willingly enough, trusting his "Kind Spirit" with all his heart. Had that been a mistake?

'I have waited long for this opportunity.' Gazing westwards, Mephistopheles's eyes took on a distant look, as if seeing through the thicket of trees and far beyond. 'An interesting man, Sir Richard, if a little lacking in – ah – resolution. Not so his foster-son. Though even he, I'm sorry to say, let me down in the end.' Pressing his lips to a thin line, he paused before continuing: 'I lent John Striven a precious gift. A Life Stone. Unfortunately, when I came to reclaim my treasure, he had mislaid it.'

Henry gasped. 'The Quintessence! He *lost* it? But it was everything to him!'

'You know much,' murmured Mephistopheles, his eyes polished smooth. 'In that case you will know where to find it. Bring it and place it in my hands. That is all I ask in return.'

In return. *For what exactly?* 'I – I'm not sure,' Henry stammered. 'I'll – I'll think it over, if that's all right with you.'

'I fear not, Master Fowst. I offer you this bargain here and now. You have longed for the chance to be rid of your troubles; will you let it slip through your fingers? Once gone I will not return.' Bowing his head, Mephistopheles wrapped his cloak around his shoulders.

'No!' Henry started forwards. All the worries of the past weeks, the effort of smuggling the sword home and steeling himself to use it, would it all be for nothing? 'Please,' he cried, 'don't go! I didn't mean— '

'Do you wish for freedom from your enemy or don't you?'

'Yes, but—'

'There is no but. That is the deal. Yes or no?'

Henry swallowed. 'Yes.'

Mephistopheles's face relaxed. 'Well-chosen, young master. I look forward to receiving the Quintessence at our next meeting. For now, farewell.' Sweeping off his hat, he made a deep bow.

Henry's mind reeled. 'The Quintessence – no, wait! How can I find it? I don't even know what it is!'

Before him the beech tree rose into the sky, branches waving in the wind. He was alone.

In the distance a dark, four-footed shape padded westwards in the direction of Northwell School.

IV

Patience is rewarded; I have my instrument. The boy suits my purpose admirably. Desire set him on the path to me; fear will keep him there.

To work, then. I to my task, you, my boy, to yours. Somewhere the stone will be lurking. Finish what was begun four hundred years ago and I will be satisfied.

CHAPTER TWENTY-FIVE

Ralph Is Indisposed

The drizzle returned, sharpening into rain. Puddles formed in the dips in the track. Head down, holding his anorak close to his neck, Henry sped towards the ring road, turning sharp left on to the foot and bicycle path. A stitch stabbed his side, forcing him to slow down. Never mind. By the number of people walking in the same direction or swishing past on bikes, he'd be in time. Out of breath, mud-spattered but who cared? He'd find some way to return the sword and – and that was it. Over.

Because the whole thing was ridiculous! This so-called bargain he'd made, to find a mysterious object never described to him, lost goodness knows where, in return for help against a person he hadn't actually identified. How exactly was the guy going to "deal with" his enemy, when he hadn't even waited to hear who he was?

Deal with. The words jarred his thoughts. Just as well he hadn't mentioned Ralph's name. There was something more demonic than angelic about this

Mephistopheles, whatever John Striven said. If he existed at all, and his own mind hadn't just been playing tricks.

Good point.

Turning, Henry let his gaze sweep over the hedge on his left, across the recreation ground, ploughed fields and water meadows beyond. There was no sign of anyone – certainly not of a black poodle. Now he thought about it, the situation was so unlikely he wanted to laugh. What, a guy in Shakespearean costume, speaking in old-fashioned language, turn up and offer to solve all his problems? Yeah, right. He'd been reading too much of the diary, that's what.

A nagging phrase rose in his memory: *when I came to reclaim my treasure, he had mislaid it*. Odd that Henry should imagine that. It would explain why John Striven disappeared from the scene after 1586, if what was supposedly protecting him from Thomas no longer did. But if so… a cold feeling crept over Henry's skin. Might Thomas have really succeeded in doing away with his foster-brother?

Crossing the river, the path left the bicycle track and cut across the water meadow towards the churchyard. Moss-covered stones glimmered in the shadow of the ancient yew, leaning at crazy angles in the long grass. Henry caught glimpses of letters carved on them as he passed; one of them might mark the grave of a boy the same age as him, his life cut short…

No. If Thomas had killed John it would be known.

Murder was murder, even if the victim was the son of a household servant, and Doctor Northwell would've had a real crime to write about instead of a vague legend about a curse. Far more likely that John's name dropped out of the accounts of Walton Hall because Thomas eventually persuaded his father to send him away.

At the corner of the churchyard the path met the main road. Henry sped along the pavement for a few hundred metres before turning left down Walton Road, right through the school gate and down the tunnel into the playground. Reaching the classroom, he pulled off his soaking anorak, hung it up and slid to his desk just before Mrs James entered. Ignoring Charlie's raised eyebrows he leaned back, feeling his cheeks burn in the warmth of the room. He'd made it.

Mrs James called the first name on the register. There was no reply. Henry looked round and something jolted inside him.

Ralph Adoney's desk was empty.

'Skiving, probably,' snorted Charlie as, a few minutes later, they made their way to the assembly hall. 'Ralph hates double maths. He'll turn up in break with a note to say he's been to the dentist or something, you wait.'

Of course. Henry grinned back at Charlie. That was, after all, the most likely explanation. Nothing to be worried about.

Maths, French, back to the classroom for break. Still no Ralph. A small knot began to tighten in Henry's stomach. This was insane! Why, having wished for his enemy to disappear, did Henry now long to see him back again?

His enemy. The word beat in his mind, echoing another voice, smooth and powerful… No, it had been a hallucination, brought on by desperation! Even then, he hadn't mentioned Ralph's name, there was no way the guy – if it really had happened and he hadn't imagined it – no way the guy could…

Wait. He'd thought him.

Henry stood still. Books and pencil case slipped from his hands and crashed to the floor.

Like he'd thought Thomas Walton.

He gripped the desk to steady himself. People rushed past, kicking his scattered pencils across the lino. Breathing deep, he forced his mind to work calmly.

Nothing happened in the thicket. He'd freaked out, that was all. Ralph being away was a coincidence. People missed school all the time.

The classroom door banged shut as voices drifted away down the corridor.

Now was the moment, quick, before anyone returned. Seizing the bundle sticking out of his book bag, he unwrapped the sword, thrust it back in the locker and closed the door. Gathering up his pencils, he plonked the case inside his desk, put on his sweatshirt and made for outside.

A figure came flying across the playground. 'Guess what! Ralph won't be back for days! Wanna know why? He's in hospital!'

Henry's fingers tightened on the door handle. The door swung back, pulling his arm. Opening his mouth he tried to say something.

'Hey, it's not as bad as that.' Charlie skidded to a halt. 'He'll be OK. Just needs a few stitches. Got attacked by a dog, apparently, on the way to school.'

'A – *dog*?' Henry's legs turned to jelly. He should let go of the handle, someone might come charging through the door any second; but his limbs refused to work properly.

'Yeah. Jake's just got a text from him.' Charlie nodded over to the far side of the playground where Jake stood amidst a cluster of people. 'Dirty great Rottweiler appeared out of nowhere apparently.'

Henry closed his eyes. At the back of his brain a shutter opened. 'A – Rottweiler?' he whispered. 'Are you sure he said Rottweiler? Not a – a poodle?'

Charlie stared at him. 'Are you nuts? A poodle – *savage* someone? What, with its tiny paws and sharp little teeth? Don't think so somehow.' Taking a marble from his pocket, he tossed it in the air and caught it. 'Go and ask Jake yourself if you like. A great, mean, slavering brute of a Rottweiler, he says. Took a great chunk out of Ralph's arm. Shouldn't think Ralph will be playing football for a while even when he does get back. Hm' – a thoughtful look crossed his face – 'wonder who'll act as team captain meanwhile? There's a match on Saturday.'

Henry let the door swing to and stepped on to the

playground. A fine rain was falling, sending drops trickling down his neck, but he felt nothing. A Rottweiler, not a poodle. Nothing to do with a poodle. He plunged his hands into his pockets, not to keep them dry, but to fight the urge to run and shout and throw his arms in the air. Which would look bad, given Ralph's injury.

'Thought you'd be grateful to that dog,' grinned Charlie. He flicked out his hand to catch the marble again. 'Want a quick game?'

Grateful. *Grateful*. More than Charlie would ever know.

CHAPTER TWENTY-SIX

The Cockerel

Walton Hall, August 1586

'John, it gladdens me that you read so much in the library but not if it brings you to neglect your foster-brother. He should come first with you.'

John's chin jerked up. His head felt still the touch of the warm, steady hand, fingers spread out in blessing. On the wall behind, a white-haired Isaac, stitched in silk, forever repeated his master's gesture, blessing one son in place of another. Beside him Thomas, eyes downcast, looked the picture of an injured, supplanted Esau, standing mute in the shadow of his scheming brother, Jacob.

The blood rushed into John's cheeks. There was no comparison! If anything, their situations were reversed, with Thomas seeking to do *him* ill! But looking up into his master's face, he felt something clutch at his heart. 'N-no sir,' he stammered. 'I ask your pardon – and Thomas's – if I have.'

'Summer days are long,' said Sir Richard. 'You should

be out on horseback together, not confined indoors. Thomas cares more for your company than you do for his, it seems.'

'Forgive me, sir,' said John. The hint of pain in his master's voice cut deeper than any rebuke could; yet how could he reveal the true state of things? 'I have been much at fault. I – am sometimes absorbed in a book and forget those about me.'

'Well then, which are these books that so' – an odd note entered Sir Richard's voice – 'so absorb you?'

John glanced upwards. His master's eyes were kind as ever; yet something lurked in their depths.

'There are works – manuscripts – in my library that are there not for – for their – *content*, but for their, ah, rarity. Even so I should perhaps…' Sir Richard's voice trailed away.

John stood still. His master's face had taken on a distant look, as if his mind were somewhere else altogether.

'Not for their content,' repeated Sir Richard, focussing on John once more, 'which to a young, inexpert mind might prove dangerous. They should not' – he coughed – '*must* not be opened.'

A quivering seized John's insides. His throat went dry. From the corner of his eye he saw Thomas watching him intently. 'Sir, I read – I read…' What? A dozen books at least he could name but for now all that filled his mind was a thick piece of folded vellum, covered in faded brown writing. Yet why? He hadn't *read* the manuscript exactly. Merely glanced at it, once! Forcing the image away, his tongue found at last what it sought. '*The Cosmographia*,' he said. 'And Pliny's *Secrets and Wonders of the World.*'

Sir Richard's brow cleared. 'So I should have guessed,' he chuckled. 'At your age I loved them too.' Closing his eyes, he pressed his finger and thumb to their sockets; open once more, they danced with amusement. 'No doubt you wish then to visit those lands where people have feet of a size they can sleep under? Or perhaps capture an Ethiopian Dragon?'

'With all my heart!' said John.

The broad shoulders shook with laughter. 'Have a care, John! These are pretty stories but it is marvellous how many learned men know of lands never discovered, or can describe a Dragon who have not seen one. Now be off, both of you' – he waved towards the door – 'and use this fine evening!'

'Come, John, we will ride!' Under his father's delighted gaze Thomas flashed a smile over his shoulder before shooting out of the chamber.

John followed, down the passage to the east wing and the tower stairs, not too swiftly. It was better to keep Thomas ahead where he could see him. His playfellow might wonder at his new strengths and skills but as long as the stone remained secret John was safe enough.

Secret… like the manuscript. At the top of the stairs John stopped.

Why didn't he confess to the manuscript? He had no

reason to think it among the ones that were not to be touched. Surely, if that were so, the master would never have left it on the lectern for him to find that day. Well, not him in particular – but he couldn't be the only person, apart from the master, ever to enter the library.

Though perhaps not many visitors would have given the dull-looking thing a second glance. And from the layer of dust it had lain there some months – years even – unnoticed, forgotten, even by the master himself.

Well, so be it. Fingers brushing the stone wall, John began to descend. Everything he'd said was true, after all. He did read much in those other books, while the manuscript itself he'd not looked at since the day he rediscovered it. No need to mention it to Sir Richard, now or ever.

From the darkness round the bottom of the stair a figure leapt out at him. '*With all my heart!*' it mocked.

Falling backwards, John struck his spine against the edge of the stone steps.

Thomas lunged towards him. 'A serpent speaks more truth than you!' he spat. '*Cosmographia*, forsooth! My father may be deceived but I'm not. I'll find you out, *foster-brother*, do not fear!' A squeak of the door and he was gone, running along the wall to the gate that led out of the herb-garden.

John shot to his feet. The fall hadn't hurt him – nothing did now – but that was beside the point. He'd like to seize that sneering, spiteful face and hurl it with all his might against…

No. Leaning against the core of the staircase, he slid his hand into his pocket, fingers closing on the smooth, cool, familiar shape. His shoulders relaxed. That was better. Just let him go. Thomas could rail and curse all he liked but that was all he could do.

Hand still in his pocket, John went outside, blinking in the sunshine. He entered the stable yard to see his playfellow aim a few kicks at the chickens pecking for grain in the dust. Oh, that one of these poor beasts might turn suddenly, giving back blow for blow!

He stopped still. With a rush of tail feathers, green, iridescent, a cockerel streaked across the yard to thrust its beak into Thomas's leg. Thomas yelped, lost his balance and fell sprawling just where recent heavy rain – mingled with horse dung – had collected in the ground. Foul liquid spattered in all directions.

John burst out laughing. This was too good to be true! A stable boy rushed to help, only to be sprayed with great gobbets of black slime, aimed not at him, but at John. 'You – *devil*!' Thomas flailed around, choking with anger. 'This is your doing, you scheming, counterfeiting, sneaking wretch!'

John opened his eyes wide. 'Why, Thomas, I was nowhere near you! I am sorry for your accident. Though to be sure, I never thought to see you brought down by a poor farmyard fowl.'

On his feet now, Thomas pushed away the stable boy. Mud clung to his silk doublet and hose and plastered his hair to his neck. From his hat the feather drooped, broken, sending black drops flying as he raged at John, as if they were the bitter words themselves given visible form. 'I – know not what – witchcraft – you practise,' he panted, 'but by God I swear – I will find you out and – and –'

John lifted his chin. 'And – what, *foster-brother*?'

'I'll – I'll –' Thomas went for his sword but instantly dropped his hand as mud squelched between the fingers, smearing the hilt. John couldn't suppress another peal of laughter. With a strangled cry, Thomas hurled himself past, back through the gate to the herb garden and up the path to the house.

John gazed after him for a moment before sauntering over to the stables. Plenty of time to tack Bramble up – which, though he could command to be done, he still liked to do himself – before his playfellow returned in a clean set of clothes.

It was unfortunate that the cockerel should have turned on Thomas like that, most unfortunate. If, while touching the Quintessence, John had happened to wish for exactly that to occur, it was a coincidence. Nothing more.

Sliding his right hand into his pocket, John smiled.

CHAPTER TWENTY-SEVEN

'The Bargain Is Made'

Henry sat up straight. He rubbed his brow, as if to smooth out any lines that had etched themselves there while he was reading.

Something wasn't right. This wasn't John talking – writing – was it? It didn't sound like him. OK, so he'd suffered enough at Thomas's hands to be allowed a little pleasure at his comeuppance. And it *was* funny, the nasty little creep being sent sprawling like that. But still... Henry's smile faded. That coolness in John's tone – bordering on calculation, almost – as he finished the entry for "*Saturday, thise twelfthe day of August*"; that was a side of him Henry hadn't noticed before. Perhaps, after all, he didn't know John Striven as well as he thought he did.

Yet what was the poor guy to do? Being nice hadn't worked. Of course he'd had to harden up a bit, even if it meant frightening Thomas out of any more murder attempts. And, thanks to the lucky charm that made him feel invincible, he'd done it.

Henry got up and stretched. Enough for now. He

didn't want to risk letting John carry him away with all that Kind Spirit nonsense, like before. What had he been thinking of, messing around in the thicket with that stupid sword? So desperate to get Ralph off his back he'd imagined this Mephistopheles person shooting across four centuries to turn up in the recreation ground – accompanied by a poodle. A *poodle*! That just proved it. His mind, under great stress, had gone haywire and conjured up all these bizarre images… well, he was himself again now. He might not have found a solution to his problems but at least he was no worse off than before.

Opening his bedroom door, he found his way blocked by a large cardboard square resting on a small pair of feet in rabbit slippers. The square quivered as it moved slowly along the landing before a dry crunch brought it to a halt.

'Rachel—'

'Won't be long.' Fingers tipped with pearl-pink nail varnish struggled with the corner stuck in the banisters, managing at last to release it.

Seizing his opportunity, Henry slipped past.

'Henry!' At the end of the landing Rachel pushed a cloud of frizz off her forehead. Next to her the cardboard square, now horizontal and teetering slightly, spanned the gap between the banister rail and the wall. 'Izzie's coming round. Can we have your duvet?'

'Sure. Whatever.'

Put Rachel Fowst and Izzie Taylor together and the

house would be a maze of tunnels and dens in no time at all. He could see them already huddled under the cardboard, surrounded by sweet wrappers, whispering and giggling. It was the perfect time for him to meet up with Charlie for a game of football.

From the kitchen came the clattering of baking dishes: Dad finishing the washing up. Henry popped his head round the sitting room door. 'See you later, Mum.'

A hand lifted and fell again at the far end of the sofa where his mum lay full length, eyes closed, newspaper across her front. He closed the door softly.

It was good to get out. His brief catch-up with John through the diary couldn't make up for the previous two hours spent with Dr Northwell (thanks to Meena's library copy, handed over as promised). The delight with which the doctor gloated over the 'primitive superstition' that had enabled him to buy the remains of Walton Hall at a knockdown price and turn it into a thriving boys' school became wearying after a while. Nor did the doctor seem interested in how the legend of the Curse of John Striven took hold in the first place. Plenty of buildings were destroyed in the Civil War, weren't they? And for fire to strike, what, three times in the following two centuries wasn't *that* unusual, surely? That kind of bad luck happened.

Or – seen the other way round – good luck. Because whatever happened to the rest of Walton Hall down the years, its heart always escaped. The library with its carved staircases, gallery, criss-cross plaster ceiling and shelves of old books all remained in perfect condition. Weird. Magical almost.

In the back of his mind a voice spoke. *Perfect, Hamface. Good to see you taking so much trouble over my essay.*

Henry quickened his pace. He didn't want to think about Ralph. He was out of the way until Monday, maybe longer, that was what mattered. And even when he returned – less than a week from the deadline – wouldn't he have trouble, with an injured arm, typing up the essay? He could hardly present one in someone else's handwriting. Bet he never thought of that.

A wild hope seized Henry. Plunging his hands in his pockets, he almost ran down the track to the recreation ground. It was possible, just possible, that Ralph might decide the whole thing was too risky.

'Well met, Master Fowst.'

Henry skidded on sand and pebbles.

The man sat, scarlet cloak spread out under him, against the beech tree by the thicket. From the tip of the long feather in his cap to the toes of his black leather boots, he looked disturbingly, solidly real. Not imaginary. Nor did the way he now got to his feet and, having brushed leaves and bits of mud off his cloak, draped it over his shoulder, strike Henry as a set of movements conjured up by his own fevered brain. His heart banged against his ribs.

Mephistopheles made an elegant bow. 'The Quintessence, Master Fowst, if you would be so good.'

'The Quin—' Henry's mouth went dry. 'I – I haven't got it.'

Mephistopheles's hand, completing the flourish of the bow, slowly descended. A line appeared on his smooth forehead. 'You have had your wish. And three days besides for what you undertook to do in return. Was that not enough?'

Henry couldn't move. His arms stuck to his sides. He opened and closed his mouth, unable to speak.

'Your enemy threatens you no more. I saw to that.' Mephistopheles's eyes seemed to sink back in their sockets, their gaze hard and cold. 'But you have not dealt likewise with me. Do you think I am to be played with?'

Trembling swept through Henry. Something clicked under his knees and he slid to the ground. 'You – you mean, it was *your* dog—'

'Mine – or rather, myself. We are the same.'

'*You can turn into a dog?*'

'There are many forms I can take, if they suit my purpose. In general a poodle is my preferred choice.'

Henry dug his fingers into the grass, twisting it in handfuls, his mind grappling for a memory he knew it held, the one fact that would stop this nightmare *now*. It came to him. 'But it was a Rottweiler!' he cried. 'Ralph was attacked by a Rottweiler, it can't have been you!'

'A Rottweiler?' Mephistopheles lifted one eyebrow. 'I can see he might have preferred that. For his own conceit, perhaps. I am well aware of the mockery which the poodle, that finest of hunting animals, has to endure in this uncivilised age.' A ripple seemed to glide across his features and they relaxed. 'Very well, your confusion excuses you. I will allow you a little longer.' He began to draw his cloak around his shoulders.

'No, wait!' Henry scrambled to his feet. 'There's been some misunderstanding. I didn't want – I never meant you to hurt Ralph! He – he'll be all right, won't he?'

No reply. The fine fingers continued to arrange the deep folds of red and black.

'W-won't he?' Henry's voice fell to a whisper.

The stillness of the figure before him sent chills down his spine. In his mind Ralph's face, white and trembling, rose up, mouth open in a scream as a great, black, snarling creature with blood-red eyes tore at his throat.

He sank to his knees. 'Pl-Please, no. Please l-leave R-Ralph alone. I don't w-want this bargain.'

'The bargain is made. It cannot be unmade. If you care about your enemy now as much as you hated him before, see that the Quintessence is placed in my hands. There are *worse* things,' the cold voice lingered, as if tracing the point of a dagger over bare flesh, 'than a mere dog bite. You have three more days.'

Henry crumpled and fell forward. Grass clung to his face and brittle, curled leaves broke on his tongue but he felt and tasted nothing, all he knew was the hammer of words echoing and re-echoing in his brain. *Bargain is made. Cannot be unmade.*

When he dared look up, the landscape around him lay empty. Only the grass under the beech tree looked flattened, as if a shape had been drawn there. A perfect circle.

V

So. It seems the boy cannot make up his mind. He wants to hurt his enemy but not cause him pain. To have him out of his life and yet not dead. I can be patient; I can also be tested too far.

It matters not to me how the noose is tightened. I use what material I have. If it's now the fair-haired boy's life that counts, not his death, so be it.

Master Fowst has failed me once; he must not do so again.

CHAPTER TWENTY-EIGHT

Suspicion

Walton Hall, September 1586

The day promised warm for September. To the east the sun outlined the distant hills and fell gold on the river. Mist curled away to reveal sheep dotted over the grass, their coats still light and soft from summer shearing. Northwards the avenue of limes stretched away to the little gate in the wall, beyond which rose the solid, crenellated tower of St Nicholas's, pale in the early morning sun.

Sir Richard quickened his pace. The slow bell calling to morning prayer had stopped and a higher, brighter chime warned them they had but ten minutes to go. They had never been late yet, slipping in by the side door reserved for the master of Walton Hall, while servants and villagers had long since gone round by the main entrance.

Dew soaked through John's boot leather as he swished through the grass. Beside him padded Flash – alone, her last two puppies now given elsewhere – the hair on her legs wet and matted, on her back shining like copper. Abel strode a few paces behind, woollen cap pulled firmly over his broad brow, cheeks and hands ruddy in the autumn sun. From John's left, Sir Richard's voice rolled down pleasantly, talking of the harvest, which had been good, of the apples, pears and quinces ripening in the orchard, of the fine hunting they would have if the weather held; and John listened with half an ear, his eye on the brambles that followed the course of the river. Matins, dinner, vespers, then at last those precious few hours of freedom and he could bring his sisters there with their baskets; already he could taste the glistening, sweet fruit bursting on his tongue, while beside him Esther and Katherine covered their hands in dark purple smears…

On Sir Richard's other side a voice spoke, as if its owner had been biding his time.

'Father,' said Thomas. 'What does it mean when a natural philosopher draws a star inside a circle?'

John breathed in sharply. He dropped his gaze to hide it from the master who – lucky for him – swung round to his son so hastily that the point of his scabbard brushed John's leg. 'What?' he said. 'Where have you seen this?'

'Why, in the library,' said Thomas. 'I came across an old manuscript…' His voice faltered.

Half-turned towards his son, Sir Richard stood motionless. John couldn't see his face but didn't need to; the fear in Thomas's eyes told all. His stomach tightened.

'Did – I – not – tell you, Thomas,' said Sir Richard, and his words came out unsteadily, as if only just under his control, 'that there are certain manuscripts in my collection *which are not to be read*?'

Thomas shrank away. 'Father, I cry you pardon! I didn't read it, I swear – I found it on a shelf of old books and just looked at the picture. How could I know it was one you wouldn't wish us to see?' He threw a glance at John, as if calling for his support.

John stood rigid, his mind in turmoil. So the manuscript *was* forbidden! And Thomas, guessing his foster-brother had been reading things he shouldn't, had sneaked into the library to seek evidence for his suspicions!

Nausea swept through him. Swallowing, he fought it down. Whatever his doubts, he must stand firm, return Thomas's look in all innocence and foil his playfellow's attempt to make him incriminate himself. Thomas might suspect but he could prove nothing. All John had to do was hold his nerve.

Straightening up, Sir Richard turned to face both boys together. 'Listen to me,' he said.

Something in the stillness of his tone set the skin prickling on the back of John's neck.

'My great love for books does not blind me to their dangers. The true natural philosopher uses the powers of reason and learning God has given him to make his discoveries. He does not dabble in necromancy.'

The sickness in John's stomach returned ten times sharper than before. *Necromancy?* The stuff of witches!

Brewing poisons from bats' wings, snake venom, dead men's bones, out of sheer spite to destroy people – what had that to do with summoning angelic assistance?

'Whoever ventures beyond these bounds,' Sir Richard continued, 'may not call what he does necromancy yet he deceives himself. Thinking he deals with angels, he ends by promising his soul to the devil. Evil charms call forth evil demons, though they may smile like angels; nor, if the bargain once be struck, can the soul be saved except by God's mercy. Believe me, I know this better than any man. Now' – he paused, breathing heavily, brows knit together – 'do I have your solemn promise that you will leave such works in the library alone?'

If his master had struck him across the face, John would have felt the shock less. This could not be true! His hand longed to close around the stone in his pocket, to feel its promise of safety, but he did not dare. No wicked demon gave him this, but a good spirit, of that he was sure! Why must the master think all spirits evil? Perhaps, persuaded by John Dee's arguments, he'd tried to summon one all those years ago and failed. Or perhaps his courage had left him at the crucial moment of accepting the spirit's gift, and now he grudged that anyone else should do so!

No. Unclenching his fingers, John let his arms fall by his sides. What was happening to him? How could he think such ill of someone from whom he'd known nothing but kindness? Who even now stood waiting patiently for his answer – and what should he say?

He stared down at the ground. Beside him Thomas

drew himself up, hands behind his back, the very image of obedience. 'Yes, Father.'

Now for it. Under Sir Richard's steady gaze John could feel the sweat softening the folds of his ruff and trickling down beneath his shirt. Yet what was there to fear? He hadn't touched the manuscript since that blessed day in July when it had yielded up its secret – here was a promise easy to give! Forcing his chin upwards, he tried to raise his eyes but instead found them directed down at Sir Richard's pale, freckled hand resting on the pommel of his sword. 'Yes, sir,' he said.

There. He'd done it. All would be well now.

No one moved. The high church bell stopped. Silence rang around them, broken only by the cooing of pigeons and the bleating of sheep.

The fingers on the pommel tightened. 'John, you have a troubled look,' said Sir Richard. 'Is there anything you wish to tell me?'

No, this was too much! He'd told the master what he wanted to hear, what more was there to say? Beside him he sensed his companion throw him a swift, hungry glance. Oh *yes*, Master Thomas, what a triumph to see his hated foster-brother give himself away!

Clasping his hands behind his back, John brought his head up in one single movement. 'No, sir,' he said.

Only then did he see the expression in his master's eyes. Not anger, not doubt. Instead an immense sadness mingled with – worse – a sense of betrayal. 'Oh, John,' he said. 'May God have mercy on you.'

A trembling seized John, he didn't know why. 'S-sir?' he stammered.

Sir Richard looked away. 'I am to blame,' he murmured. 'Valuable or no, I should have burnt the accursed thing.' Turning on his heel, he strode to the churchyard gate. Abel rushed forward to open it for his master and followed him through, shaking his head. Sir Richard did not look back.

John gazed after, a rawness in his throat. To forfeit the good will of his beloved master – that he hadn't bargained for!

Bargained for… In his mind he saw again the lithe figure leaning against the gallery railing, speaking in pleasant, even tones. *I can save you from your enemy, Master Striven. In return all I ask of you is one small thing…*

John's legs buckled. *Evil charms call forth evil demons.* The words whirled in his brain. With all his strength he fought to hold them still, to test their meaning against what he knew for certain, even while all other certainties seemed to shift and melt away. It wasn't, *couldn't*, be true. His bargain was with a good, kind spirit who wished only to protect him, entrusting him with a beautiful, precious, life-saving gift…

He thrust his hand into his pocket, no longer caring to keep his movements hidden. He needed to feel it now, that cool, solid, round perfection, clasp it in his fingers – *yes*. There it was. All comfort, all safety, all power lay now within his grasp. As they would forever, preserving his life, rendering Thomas's malice harmless, turning it back on his own head perhaps, redoubled – John's face relaxed into a smile.

Down the avenue, a few paces away, Thomas stood, staring at him. Meeting John's gaze, his dark eyes widened before he snatched them away and turning, half-ran, half-stumbled towards the gate. Ha, the tables were turned indeed!

Drawing out his hand, John followed in a leisurely fashion. He had nothing to fear. He'd keep his promise to his master, not look at the manuscript or any other such works again. Sir Richard would soon see he had no cause for concern. As for Thomas – well, let him try to undo him. He wouldn't succeed. And if he became too troublesome, there were ways of bringing him to heel. More horse manure. Or a fall, preferably into a thorn bush. A touch of the stone would do it.

Reaching the church door, John suppressed a chuckle.

No doubt about it, his Kind Spirit had done him a good turn.

CHAPTER TWENTY-NINE

The Quintessence

The pages wouldn't stay still. They trembled at the corners, making the handwriting with its long downward strokes dance. Henry let the diary fall and clasping his arms around his knees, rocked himself back and forth on the bed.

Oh John, what have you done?

This wasn't the John he knew. The boy whose problems, over four hundred years ago, foreshadowed his own so closely that he'd felt like a brother, no, more than a brother, a mirror image of himself: in the last few lines of this entry, he'd changed almost beyond recognition. Fair enough, it was good to see Thomas take some of his own medicine, but John's triumphant attitude left a nasty taste in the mouth. Let alone the lie – there was no other word for it – he told his master. And the lies he told himself!

Because now it was becoming horribly clear what a complete fool John had been. To seize on such a marvellous gift without realising he was trading his own soul – not to a good spirit, as he thought – but to the *devil*!

He stopped rocking. What about him?

He'd just done the same thing. Made a pact with the devil! So the guy never let on that's who he was but what excuse was that? It hadn't felt right, from the moment Mephistopheles appeared out of nowhere; but Henry had just gone along and let it happen! Pretending to himself it was all his own imagination, when deep down he *knew...* How could he blame John? Mephistopheles probably caught him in the same way, with those eyes that saw straight into your mind and that smooth, persuasive air.

A pact with the devil. Henry tightened his arms round his legs and brought his cheek down to his knees, hunching everything together to stem the tide rising within him – *no*. He mustn't panic. There'd be a way out, there *had* to be.

Sitting up, he breathed in deeply, letting his shoulders relax. He must just think it all through. At least things weren't so bad for him. He hadn't promised his soul, after all. What he'd undertaken was to find the stone John had lost, in return for – he bit his lip hard – a savage attack on Ralph Adoney! Yeah, he'd wanted something to happen to him. But not that. What if Ralph never recovered? What if the dog – Mephistopheles – kept attacking him until he got what he wanted?

There was only one thing to do. He must find the Quintessence. Tomorrow he'd brave Lavvy again, pretend to be browsing, scan the bookshelves... He gave a groan.

How could he possibly find it? A stone he'd never seen, lost over four hundred years ago, in a house rebuilt so often that only the original hall and library remained – it could be anywhere by now! Any one of the Walton family descendants could've come across and chucked it out, or taken it away to a new home and lost it there. If Dr Northwell himself had stumbled on an odd stone hidden among the books, well, wouldn't he have discarded it as a bit of old rubbish? This was impossible! What the hell was he going to do?

He gritted his teeth. He must try, that was all. Try his hardest. If only he had some idea of what he was looking for! All he had to go on was John's own description of the Quintessence, which wasn't much, as far as he remembered. Still, he might have missed something.

Taking up the diary again, he leafed back through the pages till he got to the day John first received "*this Stone whiche holdeth in its Hearte that Preciouse Liquid he dothe call Quintessence…*"

Hm. It sounded as if the stone was some kind of container and it was the liquid inside that mattered; could the whole thing be made of glass and transparent? He sighed. *Come on John, you might have said.*

Quintessence. Funny sort of word. Did it even exist? There was a way to find out. In the book case in the corner stood his old, battered dictionary. Pulling it down, Henry flicked through the pages.

"*Quintessence: The purest form of a substance or idea; the fifth or perfect element, believed to contain all others of earth, air, fire and water, hence the essence of Life."*

He gave a low whistle.

No wonder John felt safe with this in his pocket. A *Life Stone*. Wasn't that what people in legends always tried to get hold of, to gain immortality, rule the world, possess super powers – yeah, like John Striven suddenly able to do maths and beat Thomas at fencing! Wow, if he could get his hands on that, he'd be safe forever *and* top of the class. The Northwell Prize would be in the bag and he'd never need be afraid again, of Ralph, or Jake, or anybody.

Except that…

Except that Ralph would be in real trouble if he didn't hand the stone straight over to Mephistopheles. Henry grimaced.

The next minute he gave a shout of laughter. No, it was easier than that! It was a Life Stone, wasn't it? He could use it to cure the dog bite *and* keep it forever after, having everything he wished come true! Bet Mephistopheles never thought of that. Dad's back would recover, he'd be able to read and could go back to work and none of them would ever have to worry again.

Downstairs a door banged. A clink of crockery, the smell of toast wafting from the kitchen and Rachel's voice rising with it, 'Henree! Tea time!'

Henry gave a start. What was he thinking of? He'd got

to find the thing first! Time enough – if he found it, *if* – to think about the next step then.

He picked up the diary. Given that at some point John lost the Quintessence, wouldn't he have recorded such a dreadful event? This was his Life Stone; it never left his pocket! All he had to do was keep reading and he'd get there.

'Hen – *ree*!'

His stomach yawned. Hiding the diary under the pile of comics on his desk, he got up and stretched. Tea first. Then – back to John Striven.

★

Three-quarters of an hour and several slices of toast and jam later, he slipped back into his room, closing the door. A clumping and scuffling followed him up the stairs: Rachel and Izzie, under strict instructions to dismantle their den before being allowed near the television. Well, that should keep them occupied.

Fishing out the diary, he raced through it until, yes, here was the last entry he'd read: "*Sunday, thise twelfthe day of September*". So the next date would be – he turned the page – what, *December*?

Henry stared. The growing gaps between John's entries had bothered him for a while now; it was almost as if, the surer John felt, the less he needed – or wished – to pour out his feelings. Not necessarily a bad thing but – *a whole three months*? Would he have spent the intervening time laying traps for Thomas, laughing at his playfellow's confusion, preferring not to write such things down?

An image rose in his mind. Candlelight shining on straight copper hair ending at the nape of a pale, thin neck, bright eyes stretched wide and turned to his, a mouth half-open in excitement... that was John! That warm-hearted, eager boy who threw himself into his new life with such a will to please – where had he gone? In the last couple of diary entries Henry had glimpsed him less and less; now, after a three-month silence, would he be there at all?

Well, he'd find out soon enough. He smoothed open the page.

I am still there.

Henry stopped breathing. The blood thrummed in his ears. From downstairs rose the murmur of the television; outside his door, thumps and rustling sounds mingled with chatter as the girls set to work. The voice he heard cut through it all.

Find me.

The skin crawled on the back of his neck. He sat rigid, not daring to turn his head. 'John?' he whispered. 'Is – is it you?'

Silence. Moving carefully, Henry got up and looked round the room. Leaning on the desk he closed his eyes and breathed deeply.

There was nobody there. He'd heard nothing. However real, however strong – urgent, even – the voice sounded, it was all in his imagination. He must pull himself together and concentrate on what he had to do.

Sitting down at the desk again, he drew the diary towards him.

And in his mind the smile fell from the pale, fine-drawn face, the green eyes clouding in a look that went straight to his heart.

Find me.

CHAPTER THIRTY

The Pheasant

Walton Hall, December 1586

The thunder of hooves drew them at once to the window. Even Doctor Thorne looked up from Tully's *Epistles*, frowning at the sound of such breakneck galloping.

Thomas pressed his nose to the glass. 'It's Abel,' he said. 'Then where's my father? He should be attending him.'

John looked over Thomas's shoulder. Rounding the tower at the end of the west wing where they sat, a horse raced towards the stables, mane and tail streaming in the wind; the rider crouched low in the saddle, hatless, hair wild, urging the poor beast on. A very different Abel from the one who'd ridden out with his father and Sir Richard straight after dinner, but one hour since. John felt a tightness in his chest.

'Master Thomas, it may be nothing untoward—' began Doctor Thorne.

But Thomas was already out of the school room.

John hastened after, past the screen by the hall, bearing right down the passage where the tug of icy air told him Thomas hadn't waited to close the north door. Down the steps, across the herb garden where small bushes of lavender and rosemary huddled, stiff with frost, round to the stable yard just as Abel, panting, mud-spattered, sprang to the ground. 'My master!' he cried to Hobbs, rushing out to meet him. 'With all speed send a cart to fetch him, he has suffered a bad fall and cannot move!'

John's heart turned over. He stopped at the edge of the yard.

A few paces away, in the midst of stable boys scurrying to obey orders, Thomas stood still. 'My – my father?' he stammered. 'Where is he? How could you leave him, Abel, in such a plight?'

Abel's jaw tensed. His cheeks, made raw by the wind, flushed ruddier than ever. 'Master Thomas, believe me I would not, save that Master Striven did bid me to summon help and stays with Sir Richard until I return. Come, now!' Thrusting the reins of his horse into the hands of a groom, he strode towards the stables, echoing Hobbs's commands. 'A litter! And bandages!'

Thomas ran after, seizing his arm. 'It's not possible! My father has the best seat in the county; that he should fall – I won't believe it!'

'I wish it were not so, Master Thomas, with all my heart.' A muscle throbbed in Abel's neck. From the tautness of his pose, this enforced check to explain, however necessary, was torment. 'Nor would my master ever have fallen but for a cursed pheasant.'

'A *pheasant*?'

'Aye.' Abel's voice shook as, released from Thomas's grasp, he walked up and down, striking his fist into the palm of his hand. 'Sent by the devil himself! Or why would it come bursting from the thicket to startle poor Diamond that he reared and bucked like something possessed? To throw off his master, who loved him, and trample him underfoot' – he broke off and wheeled round. 'Quick, despatch!'

A terrible foreboding seized John. Abel, usually so loyal and quiet, watchful for his master's every need, that he should rant like a wild man – then the accident must be bad indeed. The back of his throat closed and hot tears welled up in his eyes. Brushing them angrily away, he glanced at his playfellow; and was startled to see Thomas's eyes trained on him, mouth open in a look of horror.

Stable boys drew out the cart and harnessed up the pair. Metal clinked and hooves clattered on cobbles as the horses, infected with the general urgency, tossed their heads. In the midst of all, Thomas stood motionless, staring at John, while his lips formed words without sound.

Puzzled, John looked back.

'The devil,' Thomas whispered. 'The devil.'

'What?' John frowned. 'Thomas—' he reached out his arm.

Thomas shrank from him. 'Keep away from me!' he said. Without taking his eyes off John, he backed towards the cart, now loaded up and with Abel and two grooms on board. As the driver raised his whip, Thomas cried out, 'Take me with you! I would be with my father!'

The horses fretted in their harness. Panic shot through Abel's eyes as he raised them to John's. *There is not room; and the son's distress will slow everything,* they said.

John's heart swelled within him. Coming close, he gently prised Thomas's arms from the cart. 'Let Abel go, Thomas,' he said. 'We can do nought.'

Thomas wrenched himself from John's touch with such violence both might have fallen against the cart, had it not moved briskly away. As it was, John regained his balance to see his playfellow whirl round at him. 'We!' Thomas spat. 'Nay, you have done enough. You have killed him!'

'I?' John gasped. 'I've done nothing!'

'Be patient, Master Thomas,' Abel called back. 'My master lives and, God willing...' the rest was lost in the rumble of the cart and thunder of hooves.

But Thomas clenched his fist in the air. 'Hear me!' His voice rang out across the yard. 'If my father dies it is John Striven's doing, for sure he bewitched the pheasant to startle Diamond, just as he bewitched the cockerel to attack me. He's in league with the devil!'

'*What?*' Fury erupted inside John. For his foster-brother to choose this moment, with his father gravely wounded, to launch a malicious, unfounded, wicked accusation! 'How *dare* you say such things!' His hand flew to his pocket. 'By God I'll make you pay—'

He stopped. Thomas's eyes followed his every movement. Snatching his hand away, he cursed himself at once for doing so. People nearby left off what they were doing to watch Thomas's gaze. Over by the brew house, a serving man bearing a flagon of ale paused on his way.

Taking a step backwards, John let his arm fall by his side. At all costs he must stay calm. 'No, Thomas.' He spoke slowly, keeping his voice steady. 'You're speaking wildly. The cockerel had nothing to do with me.' After all, who'd believe such nonsense? He must just hold firm.

'You lie,' panted Thomas. 'When you set him on me I thought 'twas mere spite. Now I see you were but trying your power, waiting for an opportunity to kill my father.'

A great trembling took hold of John's limbs. Inside his pocket a solid weight seemed to burn into his flesh. So he might have used its power – a little – to gain some small advantage over Thomas… but that was all! That anyone – even his foster-brother who hated him so much – could accuse him of wishing harm to the best master in the world! 'Thomas—' he tried.

'That has been your purpose since the day you set foot in this house, has it not?' Thomas continued. 'First my father; then – me.'

All activity in the yard ceased. Hot and cold fevers ran down John's body as he felt many pairs of eyes on them both, as if they were duelling in the lists. He licked his lips. 'N-no, Thomas,' he said. 'You – you know 'tis not true, 'tis your grief that speaks. I' – his voice slid upwards, out of control – 'I l-love your father.'

'Master Thomas,' Hobbs strode over, 'you are much distressed. 'Tis best you and Master John go back to the house. To your work, all of you!' he called to those standing astonished in the yard. 'This is no time for idle chatter!'

'Idle chatter, think you?' Thomas. 'When I know, and my father knows, that *Master* John, as you dub him, though *necromancer* might fit better, called up a demon who gave him a charm to destroy whom he will. See where he keeps it in his pocket!'

Horror erupted in John's soul. 'Nay, 'tis only to protect me!' he blurted out. 'My master is dearer to me than...' Too late he saw the trap. Faces around him hardened. 'It is false, I swear it!' he cried. 'I am no necromancer!'

But Thomas couldn't contain himself. 'His own words condemn him! He's had dealings with the devil! Didn't Abel say the pheasant was bewitched? What proof more do we need?'

Murmuring filled the yard. A stable boy standing nearby tightened his hands on his broom. Two others blocked the way out by road, standing there casually, as if waiting for the return of the cart and its sad burden.

John spun round. In the wintry afternoon light the walls of the stable, the brew house and dairy next to it and the tower on the corner of the east wing seemed to close in. On the other side of the yard, the gate to the herb garden stood open. Hands shot out but he wrenched himself away.

Behind, Thomas's voice rose to a shrillness that seemed barely human. 'Seize him, devil's minion!'

John hurled himself at the open gate, scattering chickens to left and right, breath rasping in his throat, every nerve tensed for the blow that would stop and drag him back.

It didn't come. Instead, Thomas's laughter, more chilling than his rage, pursued him up the path. 'Fly, coward, and hide in your hole! It won't save you, be sure of that!'

The house jerked up and down as he stumbled towards it, thoughts racing in his brain. How could Thomas accuse him of hurting the master he loved? There was all the difference in the world between using the Quintessence to cause his playfellow some small discomfiture, and making it an instrument of terrible injury. Surely Thomas couldn't really think John was in league with the devil? Oh that Abel had held his tongue! Then the cause of this unhappy accident would not have given such fire to Thomas's imagination!

At the back of his brain a voice spoke, hard and clear. *Do not blame Abel. You laid that fire yourself. Your pleasure in the stone's power lit the spark that Thomas fanned into flame.*

No. He shut his eyes tight to block the voice but the words hung in his mind. Very well, yes, he *had* misused the stone, just a little – but how could he have known the danger? And now, with the whole household after his blood, all he had to protect him was that stone whose very power looked to be his downfall! What was he to do?

Reaching the door, he seized the handle and risked one last backward glance. Strange. Surely Flash would stay by her stricken master, not run home and be waiting, still as a statue, by the gate to the stable yard? Did he pass her just now and not mark her?

He narrowed his gaze. It wasn't Flash. Framed in the opening, the creature's coat showed not golden, but jet-black, and it was larger, with a soft outline to its coat; a breed he'd never seen before. As it turned and looked at him, he felt a stab of fear.

Its eyes blazed like coals.

★

No. Henry sat bolt upright in his chair.

John didn't know. *He* was there, watching him, and the poor guy didn't know. Had no idea that Thomas's accusation came closer to the truth than even Thomas realised. Because while John might be – was! – innocent, there was nothing to stop Mephistopheles bewitching the pheasant of his own accord. A voice echoed in Henry's memory, speaking softly, almost conversationally, yet with

194

an edge as sharp as the finest blade: *there are many forms I can take, if they suit my purpose.*

Coldness gripped Henry's insides. He sat, staring down at the diary, thoughts surging thorugh his brain.

If Mephistopheles *was* behind this terrible accident, the question was, why? What could have been his purpose here? The sheer fun of seeing Sir Richard badly injured – or because he knew suspicion would land on John? Was this his way of getting the Quintessence back? He promised he wouldn't return for it until John's days were nearly over, or some such phrase – and here he was! What a cruel joke – to assure John he'd be safe for the rest of his life, and say nothing about his life only lasting another six months!

Yet Mephistopheles never got the stone. Something prevented him, just at this moment… Henry rubbed his eyes. He had to keep reading. Never mind that it was nearly midnight; he couldn't stop now.

Rising from the desk, he changed into his pyjamas and got into bed. Curled under the duvet, he reopened the diary. Finding his place again was easy enough: with its jerky, uneven lines, whole sections sloping crazily down the page, the entry for *"thise 16th day of December"* stood out from John's usual careful hand.

He frowned. It looked as if John was writing in the dark. Well, there was only one place he was likely to be right now and surely the long library windows would let in some light, even in midwinter? Perhaps not enough to reach into the recess, or wherever his hiding place was.

Turning the page, he nearly cried out. A pool of blank, yellow paper stared at him, the right-hand page half torn away, the left empty except for a few lines.

"Now I tremble in such Feare I know not what I shall do, nor can the Quintessence protect me from my Companions Accusation that by my Wicked Necromancie I have schem'd my dear Master's Deathe. And yet the Truthe is the very Opposite in that it lies in my Power to Cure him. For if I can but place this Precious Life Stone near his poor injur'd Bodie he would bee made whole again. I doubte not but that I will not be suffer'd to approache him yet must I try."

That was it? Nothing more to say if he succeeded? Did John give the stone to Sir Richard – was that why it disappeared? There were about a dozen pages left; Henry flicked through them all. Not another word. Letting the diary slide from his fingers, he sank his head back on the pillow.

Wait. One thing at least he could check. Flinging off the duvet, he grabbed Dr Northwell's *History* from his desk and leafed back to the early chapters, the ones he'd skimmed through two weeks before.

There it was:

"On Sir Richard's death in December 1586, the estate passed to his heir, Thomas Walton, who, having not yet completed his education, enrolled immediately with his tutor at Oxford University."

Henry groaned. How did he miss this? If he'd spotted the date before, he'd have realised, reading John's anguished account, how it would all end! He'd have been ready for this – this failure! John failed! Perhaps he'd run to his master's deathbed with the stone in his hand, and Thomas had grabbed it and hurled it away. Or, more likely, he'd been prevented from coming anywhere near and, distracted by grief, lost the only thing that still protected him.

Picking up the diary, Henry slid it into his book bag. So much for the help it might give in finding the Quintessence. All it had done was make him relive that terrible moment when everything around John began to unravel; yet yield no clue to what he needed to know most of all! Unless to confirm the library gallery as the most likely place to start his search.

The gallery. The recess. Leaning on the back of his chair, he closed his eyes. He must just steel himself. There was nothing there. Only, somewhere at the back of a shelf, a mysterious, long-forgotten stone. *Please let it be there. Please.*

Help me.

Henry tore his eyes open. It made no difference. His mind retained the outline of a pale, sunken face framed by red hair, not shining in the sunlight this time but dull and matted, plastered to the skin with a dark, sticky substance.

The room swayed. Henry gripped the chair so hard his nails dug into the wood. The picture had come into his head from nowhere. But he knew who it was. And the voice – how could he keep pretending to himself? Like he'd pretended Mephistopheles had never appeared, the bargain had never happened, but he had and it did and if he, Henry, didn't fulfil his side, then it would be the worse for Ralph… and now here was John Striven, injured – dying even – calling across four hundred years, begging his help! What was he supposed to do?

'John,' he whispered. 'What happened to you? Tell me how to help and I'll do it, whatever it is. Just tell me!' He stood still, every muscle tensed, listening.

No reply. The image in his mind faded, shrank, as if being drawn into a distance too far for his eyes to reach. Henry's grip on the chair weakened as a great sense of weariness washed over him. Turning, he fell on to his bed, sank his head into his pillow and slept.

CHAPTER THIRTY-ONE

Up in the Gallery

He could be back. Why not? Whatever Mephistopheles said. Bandaged, arm in a sling perhaps – but sitting there as usual, legs stretched out, eyes resting on Henry the moment he pushed open the classroom door.

But Ralph's place was empty.

'...doing fine until Sunday afternoon, we were playing on his computer and stuff.' Jake sat on his desk, staring down at his feet rocking the chair. 'Then suddenly, he collapses and his temperature goes ballistic. Infection or something. Back in hospital now.'

Henry's legs refused to move. The book bag fell from his fingers and thumped on the floor.

Charlie left the group around Jake's desk and came over. 'You OK?'

'Yeah.' Henry nodded hard. 'I'm fine.'

'Just thought maybe you were ill. And that's why you didn't turn up yesterday.'

Didn't turn up... Oh hell. 'Yeah. Um, I wasn't feeling too good. Probably am going down with something.' He coughed, scraping his throat. 'Sorry.'

'Going down with something.' Charlie searched his face. 'Are you sure that's all? It's just – well, last week I thought you'd got everything sorted… but you've been acting kind of weird ever since. Look, you would say if—'

'Yes!' Henry's answer came out louder than he meant. 'Everything's great. Stop worrying about me!' He bent to pick up his book bag, his cheeks burning hot. When he looked up, Charlie had turned away. 'I mean,' he stammered, 'thanks but— '

'It's cool.' Shrugging, Charlie went to his seat.

Henry sank down at the desk next to him, a heavy feeling in his stomach. Charlie deserved better than that. And he'd never know Henry would give anything to have spent Sunday afternoon kicking a ball around with him instead of having to fulfil a dreadful bargain he wished he'd never made.

Three more days.

★

'Meena! Take them to the library!'

'What?' Meena stopped. Behind her a tubby, bearded man in a baggy jumper and corduroys with worn patches above the knee stood blinking round the playground. Next to him a lady in a denim skirt and navy cardigan flicked through a copy of the latest school magazine. Prospective parents, definitely. This was Henry's chance.

'The library,' he repeated, taking Meena's arm and

turning her round. 'I've got to get in there and this is the perfect cover. Block Lavvy for me, just for a few minutes, *please*?'

Meena extracted her arm. She looked at him, considering. 'All right, Henry. Just don't forget: you owe me.'

Her plaits caught him under the chin. 'Actually, Professor Carter, it'd be better to see the classrooms after lunch, there'll be no one there now. Let me show you the old part of the school instead, it's really interesting.'

Henry followed at a distance, arms folded over his sweatshirt. In the library corridor he paused: from the gasps of amazement, the professor and his wife had got no further than the threshold.

'Ah yes, I've heard about this place.' Professor Carter's voice drifted back through the doorway. 'Not many schools have a perfectly preserved Elizabethan library; and isn't there a minstrels' gallery somewhere?'

'Mrs D'Arcy will know.'

Brilliant. Meena was leading them straight to the bay window. Slipping off his shoes and leaving them outside, Henry crept in their wake.

'Good afternoon.' Enthroned at her desk, Mrs D'Arcy was completely hidden by the two stout figures gazing over her head and around her.

Henry's feet made no sound on the stairs. At the top he slid into the recess, tensing his shoulders against the darkness pressing down on them, fingers of cold reaching for his heart, searching, pleading – for *what?* The image of the night before flashed across his mind and he froze, not daring to move, heart thumping against his ribs. What was happening to him? John was dead, long dead! What could he want from Henry now? 'Please, John,' he whispered, 'show me. I can't help if you don't show me how.'

He didn't expect a reply. It was a relief just to frame the words, to counter this desperate sense of need with his will to meet it, if only he could. For a moment he waited, listening; then, sitting up, he looked all along the gallery.

Nothing. There was nobody there. No pairs of eyes, red or otherwise, stared out of the darkness. Breathing more lightly, he swivelled round to face the back wall of the recess again and ran his gaze along the shelves. That one, low down by the right-hand corner, the one holding all the scruffy books; now he knew what they were. A warmth rose within him as he picked out John Striven's favourite reads, the pages crammed with monsters and wonders of the world through which he'd escaped his problems. Drawing the diary out from under his sweatshirt, he pushed it in among the books.

'Oh, a *minstrels'* gallery.' Mrs D'Arcy's voice rang out from the bay window. 'You must mean the old organ loft in the hall. It's been restored recently. Part of the rail came down a couple of years ago. Two girls got up there – quite against the rules of course – and caused a frightful accident. But all's mended now. Let me show you.'

A creak of skirts, clicking of stilettos – and Henry couldn't believe his luck. Lavvy was throwing open the double doors and leading the Carters into the assembly hall, giving him a few extra moments to achieve what he'd come here to do. Easily said! And yet, if John lost the Quintessence somewhere in the library, wouldn't the most likely place be right here, near the books he loved so much? Behind them, even, concealed in a dark, forgotten corner…

Reaching to the back of the shelf, Henry's fingers brushed a hard, round shape. He seized it and pulled. It wouldn't come. He tried with his left hand, bracing his opposite shoulder for support against the right-hand wall of the recess.

His heart turned over. The wall was moving. With a soft, sliding sound, a crack in the corner grew into a thin oblong and then to a great black square as the whole section of shelves he was leaning on swung away. He toppled sideways, his knees scraping on something hard, and fell into darkness.

CHAPTER THIRTY-TWO

The Stone Is Lost

Walton Hall, December 1586

Oh God, that this should happen now! When his need was greater than it had ever been, and his master's need – his dear master, lying close to death nearby and calling for him – what should he do? Go to him, empty-handed? Or spend vital minutes searching – in near darkness for he dared not prop open the panel – for what would of a surety save Sir Richard's life?

'Abel – somebody – find my son.' His father's command penetrated the wall behind him. 'He cannot be far away. That he is not here to wait upon my master!'

'John is in hiding, I told you,' came Thomas's voice. 'Whether he fears more his own conscience or God's vengeance, I do not know.'

This was not to be borne! Spinning round on his knees, John pressed his eye to the spyhole. Tears blurred his vision.

Sir Richard lay stretched out on the long oak table that ran down the centre of the hall. Blood oozing from a wound on his head matted his hair and stained his ruff. Patches of dried mud stiffened the cloak draped across his body for warmth, which rose and fell jerkily, as if each breath were taken in difficulty and great pain. At his side, Thomas clasped his father's limp right hand and glared at his steward.

'Whatever my son has done,' John's father replied, 'he will account to me for it. It cannot give more pain than his absence now.'

John felt his heart would break. The tension in his father's jaw, outward sign of heaven knew what poison Thomas had poured into his ear – and he not by to counter it, to let his love and grief prove the falseness of such accusations!

Turning, he fumbled for the lever on the opposite wall, barely waiting for the shelves to swing open before crawling through. There was no more time to search for the Quintessence. Too late to heal his master; yet not too late, please God, to see him once more! From behind came, not a click, but a soft thud. Did everything conspire to delay him? There, his diary lay wedged in the opening. With a ripping sound he pulled it away – no matter if half a page stayed behind – and thrust it into the book case.

Down the stairs, through the library door and down the passage, servants carrying linen and basins of water leaping back as he raced past – to collide at the screen to the hall with a gentleman dressed in black, in the act of being helped out of his dripping corner hat and cloak.

A glance into the solemn face and any remaining hope deserted him.

If Father Timothy had been called, death was at hand.

'Sir, I – by your leave!' He should fall back, give the parson precedence, but he couldn't! Heads turned as he rushed into the hall. An exclamation from his father, Thomas's mouth torn open in silent rage, then John was at his master's other side and pressing the grey, lifeless hand to his forehead. 'S-sir, for-forgive me! I never meant to deceive you. My intent wasn't evil though evil came of it, and I gained something I – I' – he glanced at Thomas – 'didn't always use well. I ask your pardon.'

A flicker in the fingers, as if they would caress his brow. Gently he lowered the hand, now wet with his tears, and pressed his lips to it. 'Would I still had it by me,' he whispered, 'just now when it could do so much good!'

He raised his head in time to see Thomas make a sudden movement. Why, he neither knew nor cared. Nothing mattered anymore. Nothing but the dear, battered head before him, whose eyes lay deep in their sockets above cheeks grey and hollow and lips that… moved.

Moved. He hadn't imagined it. He put his ear close, straining to catch the faint word.

'Books.'

'Your books – your library!' cried John. 'I'll take care of them.'

A tremor went through the hand clasped in his. Again

and again the lips pressed together, striving to form words.

'Do not force my father to speak!' cried Thomas. 'See you not how it saps his strength?'

But John didn't hear him. 'Promise –?' he guessed and felt a stab of relief as the mouth relaxed. 'Promise,' he repeated. 'I promise to look after your library with all my heart – with my life.'

A touch on his shoulder, his father's. He understood. Bending his head, he kissed his master's hand one last time and stood back as Father Timothy took his place, murmuring words of comfort and blessing.

He looked up and a sliver of ice slid into his heart. Thomas's gaze rested on him, level, unblinking. It did not move even when his father's – now *Thomas's* – steward bowed and asked if Sir Richard's body should be conveyed to lie in the great chamber.

'Take him,' said the new master of Walton Hall. 'And follow, all of you. I will come. But first I would speak to my – *foster-brother*.'

The word lingered on Thomas's tongue. As if he were savouring it.

CHAPTER THIRTY-THREE

The Secret Chamber

What the hell happened?

Henry's knees felt numb. Wincing, he shifted his position to face the piece of shelving that had given way so treacherously. He slid his hands over the wooden panelling, searching for a handle, a lever, *something…*

Nothing. Not even a crack to show where the opening had been. Sitting back, he stared into the darkness, chest rising and falling and pulse thumping in his forehead.

It didn't make sense. There must be a way back. He couldn't stay trapped here with no light, no air even. Sinking his head on to his knees, he forced himself to breathe steadily, collecting his thoughts. Trapped he might be, but he wasn't going to suffocate. The cupboard felt too large for that. Sitting up, he stretched out his arms. On both sides, with a little shuffling across floorboards, he could reach a cool, hard surface. Walls, smoothed with plaster or paint, he couldn't tell, but whatever it was it meant only one thing. This wasn't just a cupboard; it was a secret room! Built between the north wall of the recess on one side, and on the other...

A pin-prick of light cut through the darkness. Crawling to the right-hand wall, he put his eye to it. It fitted comfortably, a perfectly round hole.

'Yes, there used to be an organ up there, hence the name; but it must originally have been a minstrels' gallery.'

Henry's head fell back. Lavvy's voice, as startling as the sight from above of her steely blonde helmet of hair, sailed up to him from the far end of the assembly hall, where the Carters were gazing around at the long mullioned windows, the panelling half-way up the wall and finally at the organ loft over the door. From one small hole he could see and hear everything; a hole that must have been cut there for that purpose. In which case – he swivelled round.

On the opposite side, at the same height, a tiny, paler shaft of light entered from the library, presumably from a gap between the shelves.

Matching spyholes.

So this was it! John Striven's *"dark confin'd space where I rejoice Thomas can never finde me."* Hidden by the recess on one side, while on the other... Closing his eyes, Henry visualised the hall below. Behind the dais the wall ran smoothly, no part jutting out to give the game away, its line broken only at the window end by the doors from the library, thrown open every morning by the head as he strode in to take assembly.

The doors. Two sets of doors, with a deep space in

between. Deep enough to hold Lavvy's precious props cupboard – and still leave room for a partition and a secret chamber behind.

Turning right round, he threw himself to running his hands over the floor in small circles. He understood now. Dust stuck to his hot palms and he felt the stab of a splinter but he didn't stop. Because wasn't this the most likely spot for John to have lost the Quintessence, here, in his favourite hiding place, the perfect refuge from his enemy? Damn, how deep was it? If only there was some light!

Something slid under his left hand and he went sprawling, his chin hitting the floorboards, his right arm – touching nothing. No wall and no floor. A hole? An open trapdoor? Bending his wrist, he explored downwards, knocking against a narrow plank a little way below, attached at either end to long strips of wood extending downwards at an angle. Stairs! The chamber was even bigger than he thought. If he just leaned forward…

Crash.

Snatching his hand back, he clamped it to his pocket. Too late. With a sickening inevitability came the heavy, grinding sound of several large marbles rolling from step to step to the floor underneath.

Exclamations came from the far end of the hall. A swish of skirts, then – no! – the rapid clicking of stilettos in his direction.

Henry hauled himself round. His marbles – no way

was he going to leave them behind. Gripping the edge of the floorboards, he felt his way backwards down the stairs. Ahead of him the clicking stopped. He stiffened. Mrs D'Arcy had reached the vestibule between the two sets of doors and now stood only a couple of metres away, separated from him by the recess above and the props cupboard below. Then he grinned. Her face, as she peered into the library, must be a picture. Because the noise she'd heard couldn't have come from that quarter. Not when there was nobody there.

After a moment the stilettos retraced their clicks as Mrs D'Arcy's voice faded into the hall. 'Well, it's been *so* nice to meet you but I'm sure there are other parts of the school you'd like to see…'

Quick. At the bottom of the steps, Henry scrabbled blindly.

'….through the main door, there, yes; then Meena can take you straight to the science labs.'

One – two – at least they hadn't rolled far – three; he stuffed them in his pocket. His hand brushed a crack in the floorboards, large enough for a marble to …*yes*. Squeezing his fingers in, he pulled out a fourth. Back up the stairs and now, his vision accustomed to the dark and the thin shafts of light from the spyholes, to search again for a handle on this side. There *must* be one somewhere.

'Oh yes, Mrs Carter, your son will thrive at Northwell, especially if he's a keen reader. He will be *most welcome* in the library.'

What? Lavvy's heavily-powdered nose must have grown at least half a metre. Still, the professor's wife was buying him time. There, before him, was the back of the section of bookshelves that formed the door. On the recess side of it, he'd stumbled on the lever low down, somewhere to the left of the opening. So on this side... reaching downwards to the right his fingers closed on a knob sticking out of the panelling. *Yes*. He grasped it and pulled.

Light flooded in. Shrinking back as the book case swung towards him, he crawled through the gap, cursing whatever it was catching his right knee and sending him off balance. A soft click, the door closed behind him and he was out in the gallery recess.

No time to catch his breath. Down the steps, still half-crouching, with something sticking to his leg – a scrap of paper, so that's what it was! – peeling it off his knee and slipping it under his sweatshirt, across the floor to the door, one hand in his pocket stuffing the marbles back into their bag and pulling the drawstring—

'You, boy! Turn round *at once*!' Lavvy stood between the two flights of gallery stairs, her gaze fixed like a laser on the telltale bulge in Henry's right pocket. 'How *dare* you play marbles in here? Hand them over.'

Henry's hand flew to cover his pocket. 'Mrs D'Arcy, I wasn't playing mar—'

'Don't lie to me, boy. Give them here. Now.'

He drew out the bag. His pocket felt empty suddenly, as if a part of him had gone.

Taking the bag, Mrs D'Arcy walked over to her desk and opened a drawer.

'When can I—'

'We'll see.' The drawer slammed shut.

Out in the corridor Henry's shoulders crumpled. Not finding the Quintessence was bad enough; getting his marbles confiscated just about put the icing on the cake. Sliding his feet into his shoes, he cursed himself for not remembering to leave his marble bag with them, as before, and headed outside.

'So that's where you got to.' In the playground, Charlie called over to him. His shirt was untucked and his knees scraped with mud. 'What a waste of a lunch break.'

'Oh – um, yeah,' said Henry. 'S'pose it is.'

'Just getting in some extra practice.' Charlie nodded towards the football pitch. 'Well, I thought I'd better, you know, under the circumstances.' He looked hard at Henry.

'Under the – of course!' said Henry. 'You're captain now, I forgot. That's great.'

A pink flush spread across Charlie's cheek. 'Thanks. Well, till Ralph gets back, anyway. We need him too – only just beat Dangerfields on Saturday. Hey, what's the matter?'

'Nothing.' Henry suppressed a grimace.

Charlie grabbed his arm. 'You're not still worried about that Northwell book stuff? I thought we'd agreed, there's nothing Ralph can do! And by the amount of time you're spending in there' – he jerked his head in the direction of the library – 'I'd say the prize is yours, no question. So *stop worrying.*'

'All right.' Henry swallowed. 'I will.'

'And come and play football sometime, OK?'

'Yeah. OK.'

★

Three hours later Henry dragged his feet upstairs. The house felt strangely silent. Well, it would do, with Rachel over at Izzie Taylor's for the afternoon and Dad holed up in the front room – preparing himself for the next day, according to Mum. Something important was happening then but Henry couldn't think about that now. All he could do was go over and over in his mind what he was going to say to Mephistopheles the day after.

Look, I tried, OK? I looked everywhere. It wasn't there. What more can I do?

Reaching his bedroom, he pushed open the door, suppressing a groan. He'd never be able to say that. It would cut no ice if he did. One day down. Two to go. And then? Oh come on, what's the worst that could happen? People didn't die from dog bites. Not unless the animal had rabies and there'd been no suggestion of that.

Dropping his school bag, he reached automatically into his right pocket before remembering there was nothing to take out. Damn. He threw himself down on the bed and stared up at the ceiling, following the cracks in the plaster. No marbles. No Quintessence. Nothing to show for his frantic searching in the library except a secret chamber, also empty.

Wait. Swinging his legs round to the floor, he leaned forwards and grabbed his bag.

There it was: the scrap of paper that had stuck to his knee as he crawled out of the chamber. Three roughly straight edges and a fourth, torn; it could have been ripped from an exercise book if it hadn't been so thick, so yellow…

His fingers trembled. Sitting back on the bed he gripped the scrap with both hands to hold it steady, while his eye ran along the broken edge, matching it to the torn, blank diary page lying open in his mind.

He turned it over.

"MERCY"

Scrawled in large, crude letters, far too large for a pen, more like – a finger. Like the sort of painting Rachel used to do at playgroup.

And yet not. There was something unnerving about the thick, uneven strokes, sliding into great smears and blotches: as if this one word had squeezed every last drop of strength from the writer's body.

Every drop.

An image flashed into Henry's mind. His fingers tightened around handfuls of duvet.

A red-haired boy his own age, alone, shivering in his dark hiding place, no pen, no paper save half a page torn from his own diary, no ink but his own blood – and no Quintessence to protect him. Or why would he need to plead for mercy?

The question was: *who was he writing to*? Thomas? Or Mephistopheles?

CHAPTER THIRTY-FOUR

The Walton Papers

Put it back.

Only the eyes moved in the bloodless face. They followed him as he shrank away, hands running over floorboards and wall, searching…

Put it back. There is no safety.

He must get out – he couldn't breathe. At last, the lever, his fingers round it, pulling, the wall sliding into him, the slumped figure at his feet dissolving in darkness…

Except that it wasn't a lever. It was a hand, slippery with blood.

Henry's mind shot to the surface. Lying back on the pillow, he gulped air, his throat dry, his heart thumping. Night settled into familiar shapes: desk jutting out from under the window, dark mass of wardrobe in the corner.

Only a dream, thank goodness. Only a dream.

Towards morning he woke again, the words ringing in his ears. A scrap of paper, that was all, which he never meant to take – why should it matter so much? In his mind he saw it lying still in dust and darkness, undisturbed until he'd blundered in, sending it skidding across floorboards, crushing it under his knee…

He sighed. Ok, he'd put it back. Not in the chamber but somewhere nearby, next to the diary, even – surely that would do. In a few days, that was. Give Lavvy time to… time to…

With a jolt he was wide awake. The face had turned to him with the same lifeless stare. Only the hair was blonde, not copper, and the eyes were blue.

★

He'd got to find the Quintessence! There was no other way! If Ralph died…

No. Henry dug his fingernails into his desk. *Ralph isn't going to die. That was just a dream.*

Straightening up, he tried to focus on Mrs James, sitting at the front of the class. It had cost him all his concentration not to miss his name during the register; now that was over, she was still speaking but he could make out none of her words above the clamour in his head.

Closing his eyes, he forced his thoughts to run calmly. He had till Wednesday. Yes, but what then? Oh, if only John had described the moment he lost the Quintessence! There'd be something to go on then. Or if not him, maybe someone else, noticing his distress, might have left some sort of record, a letter maybe…

A letter. An Ancient Record. Of *course.*

'Yes, Harry?' A sea of faces, all turned in his direction. Beyond them Mrs James fixed him with her eye, her chin pointed upwards, as if she'd broken off in mid-speech.

'Uh—'

'Your hand is up. I hope you're not going to ask why, under the circumstances, we couldn't possibly hold Mr Adoney to his promise for the Northwell Prize?'

Henry dropped his arm, unclenching his fist. Weird. He didn't know he'd clenched it. 'No. Um. Sorry, Mrs James.'

'Bit tactless, Henry,' Charlie murmured, as the classroom emptied for assembly. 'I know you're still angry with Ralph; but *blood* poisoning…'

Henry's stomach turned cold. 'He's got – blood poisoning?'

'Didn't you hear? I thought that's why you punched the air.'

'*Punched the air*?' Henry gaped. 'I – I didn't. Not on purpose. I – I guess I wasn't listening.'

'Wasn't *listening*?' Charlie stared. 'What the hell's the matter with you these days? You don't play football, you've got no time for marbles, you're in the library all the time working like a maniac, you're so caught up in your own world of books and prizes and laptops that you don't even notice when someone's dangerously ill—'

'No, no, it's not like that!' cried Henry.

'– I'll tell you something, mate.' Charlie walked to the door. 'There are more important things in life than a lousy, stupid laptop.'

'*Charlie* – hey!' Rushing to the door, Henry felt a shoulder slam into his, knocking him into the anoraks hanging on the wall.

'You little creep.' Jake pressed his face so close Henry shrank back, hitting his head on one of the coat hooks. 'You think the mess Ralph's in is funny, do you? And that he could die – that's funny, is it?'

'No.' The features before Henry swam out of focus, hurting his eyes. He screwed them shut. 'I didn't mean—'

'You better not,' Jake spat.

A squeak of lino, a yank of the door handle and the air in front of Henry's face felt blissfully clear and Jake-free. Opening his eyes, he let out a long breath.

Get through the day. That was all he had to do. Never mind Jake. Or – he bit his lip – Charlie. Just make it to the end of school.

Then for the town library.

★

'I'll be really careful. I don't know how far the Walton Papers go back but if there's anything from 1586 or just after, anything at all…'

She was listening. That was something. Not a straight no, like before. But then this time he could sound as if he knew what he was talking about and – more importantly perhaps, from the way the town librarian looked him up and down – had remembered to wash his hands on the way out of school.

'Well…' She tapped a pencil thoughtfully on the desk. Her gaze drifted towards the computer screen.

'Could you – could you maybe just look and see?' said Henry.

Her fingers moved over the keys. 'The Walton Papers,' she read, 'a collection of documents dating from the early 1600s to 1646 – oh dear, that sounds a bit too late for you.'

Henry sighed. Of course. Why should all the dates work out?

'Discovered in 1919,' continued the librarian, 'during alterations at the Parsonage, St Nicholas's Church, Walton, and deposited in the City Library in 1922. Well, at least you know. Sorry.'

Something stirred at the back of Henry's mind. St Nicholas's. Where Sir Richard and his family were walking that dreadful Sunday in September, 1586.

He leaned forward. 'Could I look anyway? There's this footnote in the *County History*, something about Walton Hall being an accursed place, and it refers to the Papers.'

She raised her eyebrows. 'Really?'

'Yes. I thought it could be interesting. For my essay?'

'Good for you.' Her eyes, narrowed slightly, rested on him. 'Tell you what, I'll go and have a look. If I find anything, I may be able to let you have a photocopy.'

'Uh – thanks.' He smiled. *Don't knock it*, he thought. *Better than nothing.*

The Ancient Records section seemed to be a long way

away. His gaze wandered down the length of the library and back to the desk with its notices, files, display of leaflets – and stopped. A swift glance around him – *oh come on, who's going to care?* Reaching out, he stuffed a leaflet in his pocket.

'You're absolutely right.' Out of breath, an odd note of excitement in her voice, the librarian was back.

Hope soared within Henry. 'Am I?'

Laying a sheet of paper on the desk, she pointed to the date. 'Here's the first letter in the collection, 22nd November, 1602, from the Reverend Timothy Liddell to Sir Thomas Walton, asking for help with repairs to the church roof. The vicar obviously kept his own copy. We don't have Sir Thomas's answer but it seems not to have pleased the Reverend. Do you see? Across the bottom he's scrawled: *"A wasted effort. Nothinge good will ever come from that accurs'd place."* There's your reference! Looks like a fit of temper to me.'

A fit of temper. That was it? The curse hanging over Walton Hall, all down to a spot of bad feeling between the mean-spirited master – ha, no surprises there! – and the vicar of the local church?

Henry bent to pick up his book bag from the floor beside him. So much for being absolutely right. Nothing about John Striven. Nothing about the Quintessence. A dead end, like everything else had been.

'Wait,' said the librarian. 'That's not the best bit. I turned the letter over.'

'And?' Henry's heart beat faster.

With a flourish, she laid a second sheet of paper next to the first. 'He used the back of an older letter, one to the bishop! Whoever catalogued the Walton Papers – some time ago now, of course' – she coughed –'didn't notice. But look at this date here.' She rested her fingers at the foot of the page: *Writ thise tenth day of Januarie, 1587.*"

Henry gripped the wooden rim of the desk with both hands. The long curls and strokes of the handwriting – more even and confident than John's – danced on the page.

'Such an exciting find!' she exclaimed. 'It's quite tricky to read but it seems to be about something that happened at Walton Ha—'

Henry didn't wait. Seizing the photocopies, he stuffed them into his bag and made for the door. Recollecting himself, he turned. 'Thank you!' he called back down the library. Dark looks popped over the tops of reading desks. 'Thanks!' he repeated, more quietly, and charged out into the night air.

CHAPTER THIRTY-FIVE

The Visit

The bus didn't move. Street lamps gleamed on the cars that snaked northwards down the road, all the way to the distant traffic lights. Henry sat hunched over his school bag, trying not to drum his feet on the floor. It was rush hour; what did he expect? He'd get home eventually. No point in working himself up.

The engine jerked into life and the bus crawled a hundred metres or so. Gaps appeared in the glitter of brake lights ahead. Henry watched as Walton Road – empty of Northwell pupils at this hour – opened and closed on his right and the pale stone tower of St Nicholas's church drew nearer. Soon the turn east down the ring road, and with luck he'd be home in twenty minutes; still time before supper to dive into his room and read the document.

He suppressed a groan. They were slowing down again, stopping – *no, not here*. Please, not this wide, tree-lined avenue, halfway between Walton Road and the traffic lights, where gravelled drives could be glimpsed through wrought-iron gates, leading to great double-fronted houses beyond. He wouldn't look. Even if he did, Ralph's house probably wasn't visible from here anyway.

Yes. There it was. No lights in the windows, no car in the drive, just – empty. Closing his eyes, he could see Ralph's mum opening the front door into darkness, barely able to drag her feet over the threshold, while his dad followed, silent, grim-faced.

Henry slumped in his seat, biting his cheek until pain and the taste of iron spread through his mouth. He stared down at his hands gripping the bag on his lap. It would all be OK. Ralph would be OK. He was in hospital, wasn't he? Never mind Mephistopheles and the Quintessence; the doctors wouldn't let him die. They'd be pumping him full of antibiotics, pulling out all the stops; if Henry turned up now he'd probably find Ralph lying there quite happily, loving the fuss going on around him.

Or pale, unconscious, breathing with difficulty…

Turning right at the ring road, the bus gathered speed. Henry's stop came into view; beyond it, red lights winked all the way up the road towards the hospital, a blaze of lights at the top of the hill. Another ten minutes and Henry would be there.

When the bus pulled up at his stop, he stayed in his seat.

★

'Are you one of the family?' A nurse in navy blue uniform held the door half-open.

Henry blinked. In the brightly-lit room behind her, hospital beds jutted out of a mass of screens and cables and plastic tubing looping from machines on the floor or dangling from gantries above. Everything was grey or black or sea-green.

Moistening his lips, he said, 'No, I'm – Ralph's friend. Please,' he added, as a guarded look came into the nurse's eye, 'I'd really like to see him. Just for a moment.'

'I'll have to check with his parents.' Standing aside for him to enter, she let the door click shut. 'Wait here.'

'Who's that? Someone for Ralph?' A slight figure emerged from a room on the left and looked about her.

Henry gulped. The Mrs Adoney he remembered was elegant, well-dressed, with shining blonde hair framing her smooth, unlined face; in the tired, crumpled-looking woman clutching a half-drunk mug of tea he barely recognised her. 'Hallo, Mrs Adoney,' he mumbled. 'I – I don't want to disturb you, or – or Ralph or anything, I was just wondering how he's doing…'

A warmth came into her eyes. 'It's – Henry, isn't it?' She managed a smile. 'I'm so glad you've come. Ralph needs his friends right now. Wait, I'll just get rid of this.' Turning back into the sitting room, she reappeared without the mug and took his arm.

The nurse walked ahead of them. Mrs Adoney led Henry past three beds, stopping at a fourth, half-hidden by a curtain. At first he could make out only one human shape: Ralph's dad stretched out in a low chair, head flung back, his chin and neck peppered with stubble.

'He's exhausted,' whispered Mrs Adoney. 'First sleep he's had in twenty-four hours. I keep telling him' – her voice cracked – 'we can't both stay awake, just in case Ralph—' she broke off.

Beside Mr Adoney, and barely visible under the tubes and wires running into his arms, chest, up his nose, into every possible part of his body, it seemed, lay a still, pale figure under a white coverlet. Two monitors above and to his right hummed and beeped, different-coloured jagged patterns running across their screens.

A crater opened somewhere in Henry's insides. He looked at Ralph's head on the pillow, face half-covered in tape keeping the respirator tube in place, and couldn't move.

Mrs Adoney let go of his arm. 'You can go closer,' she said. 'Talk to him. The drugs are keeping him asleep but he – he may be able to hear. That's right, isn't it?'

'Definitely.' A nurse typing on a keyboard nearby smiled. 'Take his hand, if you like. Just be careful not to touch the arterial line.' She indicated a tube inserted into Ralph's wrist.

Henry's legs felt like lead. Dropping his school bag, he forced himself to the bed. 'Ralph,' he whispered. 'It's me, Henry. I – I'm sorry…' his voice failed. Swallowing, he tried again. 'You're going to be all right. You'll get through this, I promise. Just – hold on in there.' He laid his hand on Ralph's arm.

No response. Or perhaps a flicker – slight, barely perceptible – under the closed eyelids.

A movement from the chair by the bed. Mr Adoney jerked awake and looked at Henry uncomprehendingly before his gaze flew to his son's still form. 'Ralph?' Clearing his throat, he said more loudly, 'How is he? Any change?'

'Not yet.' As Henry stood back, the nurse inserted a syringe into an opening in the arterial line. 'I'm just taking a blood sample to check his oxygen level. Try not to worry, Mr Adoney.'

'This is Henry, Malcolm,' said Ralph's mother. 'You remember? He's come to see Ralph.'

'Henry – ah, the boy who gave me the idea about the Northwell Prize,' said Mr Adoney. 'Not that I give a damn about that now.' His gaze slid back to Ralph's face.

Henry drew away from the bed. 'I've got to go,' he said. 'There's – there's something I have to do.'

'Of course.' Mrs Adoney tried to smile but her mouth wouldn't work properly. 'It was good of you to come. Ralph's lucky to have a friend like you.'

Henry nodded, cheeks burning, unable to reply. Grabbing his bag, he fled.

CHAPTER THIRTY-SIX

The Parson's Letter

'*There* you are.' Mum leaned her head against the side of the door. 'I was starting to worry.'

'Sorry.' Squeezing past her into the passage, Henry pulled off his anorak. 'I went up to the hospital. To see Ralph.'

Shutting the door, Mum let her arm fall slowly. 'Oh, that poor boy. I heard last night he'd been admitted. How was he?'

'Not good. Just lying there, tubes everywhere… Mum, he'll be all right, won't he?'

'Well…' closing her eyes, she nodded. 'They'll do everything they can. He's in the best place, that's the main thing. I'll try and look in on him before my shift. Now come and see Dad, he's feeling a bit—'

'Later!' Henry was already halfway up the stairs, unzipping his school bag. 'There's something I have to do first.'

'Henry, *please*—'

Her voice held a note that should have warned him but Henry couldn't wait. He'd been carrying the parson's letter round for hours – couldn't he grab five minutes now to look at it? 'Won't be long, I promise!' Closing the bedroom door behind him, he reached into his school bag and drew out – not the photocopied document but a small, crumpled leaflet.

Henry stood still. His mind, turning through a kaleidoscope of images, rested on his dad's face, his mum's words of yesterday – *he's preparing himself for tomorrow* – ringing in the background.

Assessment Day. Dad had been given his assessment. That's what Mum had been trying to tell him just now.

The parson's letter would have to wait a bit longer, that was all. Leaflet in hand, Henry went back downstairs. 'Dad?'

The front room door stood shut. No sound from the television. From the crunchy smell of baking potatoes coming from the kitchen and the chattering, Rachel was in there, helping Mum cook supper.

Henry stood for a moment, letting his eye run down the cracks in the brown paintwork. Then, taking a long breath, he opened the door. 'Hi, Dad.'

In a long-sleeved shirt – only slightly frayed at the cuff – and his good pair of trousers, Dad sat on the sofa, a can in his right hand. He stared at the green rectangle of the television screen, on which a white dot glided silently, colliding with several red dots and sending them rolling away in a perfect fan shape. 'Works better without the sound,' he muttered without looking up. 'More – restful.'

'Yeah.'

'Had enough of people talking at me for one day.'

Henry closed the door and edged forward. 'It – it didn't go well then, the assessment. That's – that's really rubbish, Dad, I'm sorry.' He cleared his throat. 'But I've got someth— '

The knuckles round the can whitened. 'They think' – Dad's gaze stayed fixed on the screen –'I'm depressed. Yes, that's it. And I should see my doctor. Hmm.' Putting his head on one side, he nodded slowly.

Henry held his breath.

'Depressed, of course I'm depressed! I can't do the one job I'm fit for!' The can bent in his dad's hand. '*Vocational Rehabilitation*. Nice words. Nicer than, here you are, Mr Fowst, this way to the scrapheap.'

'No, Dad!' Tears welled up in Henry's throat and stung his eyes. Oh great, that was all he needed! He blinked furiously. In his hand the shiny leaflet felt limp. 'Look at this,' he said, smoothing it out. 'I found it in the library. Adult literacy classes. There were loads of them,' he rushed on. 'There's a number you can ring – no listen!' he begged, as his dad glanced at his hand and looked away. 'Don't you see what it means? It's *not just you*! Lots of people have trouble reading. It's called dyslexia. No one believed it existed before – but it does!'

His father sat rigid, looking straight ahead, his mouth set hard.

Henry waited, hand still outstretched, while the silence grew; finally he dropped his arm. 'Please Dad,' he whispered. 'You said yourself it's *not trying* that makes – that makes –' he couldn't say it. *Failure.* The word hung unspoken in the air.

Dad switched off the television. Letting his hands fall between his knees he bowed his head. 'It's different for you, son,' he said after a moment. 'You're young. You can – change things.'

Henry flung his arms round Dad's neck. 'So can you! It's not too late, that's what the leaflet says!'

Dad's shoulders trembled. Reaching up a hand, he grasped Henry's and held it for a moment. At last he looked up, eyes moist. 'You're a good lad,' he said. Gently shifting Henry's arm, he nodded at the leaflet. 'You can leave that here if you like.' Picking up the remote control, his gaze returned to the television.

A flicker of hope. 'So will you…' Henry began.

'I'll give it some thought, son.' Dad nodded. 'I promise.'

He won't though, thought Henry, closing the door behind him as Rachel burst from the kitchen to announce that supper was ready. *He just won't.*

★

Back in his room half an hour later, Henry drew the parson's letter from his bag. It might be completely irrelevant, he knew that; but the date – 10th January 1587 – so close to John's last diary entry…

*"Your Lordship knows that on the 18th day of December laste I
was call'd to the Death bed of Sir Richard Walton…"*

He nearly cried out loud. This was it! Somebody who'd
been there and, judging by the letter's length, written a
detailed account! If anyone could throw light on what
happened to John Striven, it was the Reverend Timothy
Liddell.

Henry took a deep breath. He mustn't rush this. The
writing wasn't as clear as John's; it would need all his
concentration. Smoothing the letter flat, he sat down
and began to read.

Some minutes later, he got up and walked round the
room.

It wasn't the Reverend Timothy's fault. And it wasn't
exactly unexpected. But to read the parson faithfully
reporting Thomas's tale of how his *"Wicked foster-brothere
conjur'd up a Demon to startle Sir Richards Horse and soe did
Kill him"* was unbearable. The whole story of John
Striven's *"Sorcerie"* set down on paper for the bishop and
who knows how many others to read, laying the
groundwork for the Curse of John Striven that would
cling to Walton Hall for generations to come… Well,
he'd wondered how that rumour had taken hold. Now
he knew.

Flinging himself back in the chair he read on.

*"It seems that shortlie after his master's deathe yonge
Striven in most Treacherous wise did set upon his foster-*

233

brothere forcing him to draw his own Sworde in defence.
Whereupon by Thomas Waltons Account the thwarted
Necromancer conjur'd up a Spelle to vanish into the Air.
I feare young Waltons senses may have been affected by
Grief howbeit tis Certein John Striven hath not been seen
alive since that day, nor his Body founde that it might
receive Decent Buriall, to the grete Comfort of his
Sorrowing Father and Familie besides."

Henry let out a long breath.

So. He'd done it. Thomas Walton had finally achieved
what he'd been trying to do all along: kill his foster-
brother. Of course he'd say he was only acting in self-
defence. And after the cockerel incident (*oh John, you
fool!*), he might have genuinely held John responsible
for his father's death. Firm grounds for taking revenge
into his own hands as far as Thomas was concerned. But
what a cruel stroke of luck that he should catch John at
his weakest moment, with no Quintessence to protect
him!

Unless it wasn't luck.

Unless he knew.

CHAPTER THIRTY-SEVEN

One Last Day

I cannot rest.

Zipping his anorak right up to his neck, Henry turned his face into the wind. His hair whipped backwards and the rawness made him gasp. Good, *good*. Anything to drown the voice in his mind.

Return what you have taken.

OK, OK, he had the scrap of paper with him, he'd get it back to the library today somehow, just give him a break!

Let it lie where it fell.

On his right, cars streamed down the ring road, their line broken by buses, brightly lit windows beckoning; yet at least here, walking along the cycle path, battling with the wind, he could thrust that gaunt face to the back of his mind, not see it in the pattern of twigs in the hawthorn, in the flash of water filling the ruts on the edge of the track…

Hidden it cannot harm.

He closed his eyes. *John, I'll do it*, he promised silently, *I'll put it back. I never meant to take it away in the first place.*

Here was something he could set straight, at least! One piece of this whole awful chain of events he could put right. As for the rest of it…

His eyes flicked open. The wind stung, filling them with water. Blinking hard, he scanned the fields to his left, turning to follow them all the way back to the recreation ground. No sign of a black dog. Or of the swirl of a black and scarlet cloak. For now.

Leaving the cycle track, he cut the corner of the meadow around the churchyard, the low stone wall and tower beyond jerking with the unevenness of the path. Bare chestnut and oak trees rose up ahead, the boughs of the great dark yew swaying against the sky.

Find me.

He looked round. This time he could have *sworn…*

There was nobody there. In the distance cyclists, heads bent, pedalled into the wind. Above the fields pigeons sailed and fell.

Turning, he carried on, more slowly now. Dry, frosted leaves crunched underfoot. On his left the low wall ran smoothly, head stones beyond gliding past, here and there splashes of snowdrops dappling the ivy in the ground around them. At this gentle pace, the patterns of strokes and flourishes on the stones arranged themselves into words and phrases. *"Here lie the remains of…"*

He halted. On a tall, lichen-blotched gravestone, its top engraved with half a dozen lines, a single name stood out: *"EDWARD STRIVEN".*

Henry started forwards.

> *"sometime Steward of Walton Hall,*
> *who departed this life the 14th day of*
> *January 1596, aged 57 years. Also of SARAH*
> *his wife, who departed this life the 3rd day*
> *of November 1596, aged 47 years. And of…"*

Blood drummed in his ears. He read on eagerly, hungrily – and stopped. Shrugging off his school bag, he scrambled over the wall.

Closer to, there could be no doubt. The writing on the grey-green surface had ceased. Lichen prickled his fingers as he ran them over the stone, finding nothing. No trace of a name carved and half worn away: it had never been carved at all.

Frowning, he sat back on his heels. *"And of JOHN his son"* should come next. Or rather, the engraver should have begun with John, since the bloody encounter between him and Thomas described in the parson's letter had taken place ten years before. Not left a gap at the end of the inscription, waiting to be filled.

Waiting.

A gust of wind blew down Henry's neck. Turning his anorak collar up, he shivered.

It could just be a mistake. Or maybe someone else was intended to fill the gap – one of John's sisters, say – while he lay in another grave. That was the likeliest explanation. Given time to search the churchyard, Henry could probably find them all.

Ivy stirred at the foot of the stone and he caught his breath. The engraver hadn't finished! A curl, marks in the mottled surface… Pushing the dark leaves down with both hands, he stared at the worn letters.

They spelt a name all right but it wasn't John's, and as for the numbers following it – ah, of course. This was a churchyard, after all. *"Luke 15: 24"* referred to the bible. Some verse about resting in peace, probably.

★

Racing to the head of the queue, Henry bolted down his shepherd's pie and was out of the dining room in fifteen minutes. That left an hour to search for the Quintessence – but how to get up to the gallery this time? He couldn't ask Meena to cover for him again. And Charlie… Henry grimaced. After the misunderstanding yesterday, Charlie was hardly likely to be sympathetic.

Pushing open the swing doors at the end of the dining room corridor, he jumped back. Another centimetre and he'd have struck the two figures standing there, one with hands on her hips, the other looking about him with a distracted air. What were they doing, arguing at the top of the steps?

'I told you, Lavinia, I haven't got it. Clarissa – er – agreed to return them for me. She's the one you should be asking. Now I'm sorry, but— '

'Mrs James gave me *two* swords.' The librarian's voice was crisp. As were her heels, clicking down the steps in pursuit of Mr Johnson. 'But I lent you *three*. One is still out in your name and I would appreciate it if…'

Henry didn't wait to hear the rest. The sword, forgotten in the locker in the corner of the classroom! It was the chance he needed.

Five minutes later he stood in the doorway of the library, heart pounding. 'Mrs D'Arcy? Mr – Mr Johnson asked me to return this.' He held out one arm, keeping the other folded carefully across his front, feeling the soft crackle under his sweatshirt.

Mrs D'Arcy came forward. 'Goodness, that was quick,' she said, taking the sword. 'Thank you, er –'

'Henry.'

'Henry.' Closing her eyes, she nodded. 'I knew Mr Johnson would find it. Eventually. Thank you, Henry,' she repeated. 'I'll see to this now.'

Half-turning, as if to go, he watched to see if she would… *yes*. Making for the props cupboard, Mrs D'Arcy pushed open the double doors and for a moment, disappeared from view.

He slipped up the stairs to the gallery. Crouching low, he drew the paper scrap out from under his sweatshirt and slid it into the shelf where he'd pushed in the diary – not too deep, he couldn't risk touching the lever, not now with old Lavvy opening the props cupboard just down below. 'Please John,' he whispered. 'I've done what you wanted. It's not in the chamber but it's really close – and it's back with your diary.' Crawling, he ran his hands along the floorboards inside the recess, then out along the gallery, exploring gaps in the bookshelves, anywhere dark enough for something to hide for years, centuries, even. 'Now help me. Show me the Quintessence. I've got to find it. *Please.*'

'Just *what* do you think you're doing?'

He slid round. Hands on hips, Mrs D'Arcy looked up at him with a face like thunder.

'S-sorry, Mrs D'Arcy,' he stammered. 'I was – I was…' what? He scrambled through his brain. 'I was looking for – um…'

The squat figure took a deep breath. Its blouse seemed in danger of coming apart at the seams.

'… a bible,' he managed.

'What?' Mrs D'Arcy's arms drooped as her breath rushed out, giving a fleeting impression of a deflating, multi-coloured bouncy castle.

Henry seized his chance. 'A bible,' he repeated, hurrying back along the gallery and down the stairs. 'I thought it might be up there because it's a really old book. I wanted to look something up. Sorry. I should have asked.'

'Yes, Henry, you should.' She regarded him, head on one side. He looked earnestly back at her. *See,* his gaze said, *I can't be that bad, can I?*

Mrs D'Arcy smoothed down her skirt. 'Follow me.' Walking over to a book stack, she drew out a thick, heavy volume with a shiny dust jacket. 'Now what did you—?'

'Luke 15:24.'

'Goodness, you *do* know your references. Let me see, St Luke's gospel…' She leafed through the pages. 'Ah yes, the Prodigal Son. The young man who leaves his father for years but at last returns and begs his forgiveness.'

A great lump rose in Henry's throat. Warmth rushed into his eyes and he snatched them away, blinking. From somewhere far off came Lavvy's voice, unusually gentle. 'It *is* a lovely story.'

He stared back at her, hearing nothing. A vast, grey-green slab yawned before him, emptier than anything Lavvy or he or anyone else could know, emptier than sorrow. For now he knew why the engraver broke off where he did, leaving the stone smooth, unfinished, blank.

'Are you all right? You're not ill, are you?'

Henry shook his head. 'Fine,' he said. 'I'm fine.'

The pale face rose in his mind, eyes pleading in a way he at last understood. He pressed his fists together until the knuckles whitened. *John, if I could find you I would,* he whispered inside himself. *With or without the Quintessence, it doesn't matter. I'd put you where you belong.*

Mrs D'Arcy bent to look into his face. 'Wait – aren't you the boy with the marbles? Look, I've had them long enough.' Taking a key from the desk, she walked round and unlocked a drawer.

His heart leapt. How could he have forgotten? 'Th– thank you, Mrs D'Arcy,' he stammered, taking back the precious bag.

'I thought that would cheer you up. Not in the library again, though, please.'

'I promise, Mrs D'Arcy.'

He was still nodding when she closed the heavy door on him. But as he turned down the corridor, the smile left his face.

That was it. His last chance. Three days were up and he hadn't found anything.

Not John. Not the Quintessence.

CHAPTER THIRTY-EIGHT

The Dark Marble

Wind ruffled the puddles in the playground. A few people kicked a ball around, watching it sail far beyond their strength, or bounce back in their faces. Against the classroom block a boy leaned with folded arms, mouth set hard, pasty skin rendering his spiky hair a dirty yellow colour. Catching Henry's eye, Jake scowled. On his own, without Ralph, he cut a solitary figure.

'You got them back!'

'Wha-?'

Meena, shivering in the cold air, sweatshirt sleeves pulled down over her hands. 'Your marbles,' she pointed at the bag. 'Now you can play me.'

'*You*? Meena, you don't—'

'I do now.' She held up a closed fist. 'I bought these. I want to beat my brothers. You can show me how.'

Out of the corner of his eye Henry saw Jake drop his arms and straighten up. 'Not now,' he murmured. 'Later maybe.'

'Yes, now!' she said. 'You owe me, remember. Come on.'

Jake left the wall and walked towards them. 'Not a good time, Meena,' Henry repeated. A group of people emerged from the dining room to the right and hurried down the steps, making for the classroom block. If he headed that way, he could mingle with them and dodge Jake.

'Wait, don't go!' Meena's hand shot out, jerking the marble bag from his grip. It fell, bursting open on the ground. 'Henry, I'm sorry – here, I'll get them.' Bending over the tarmac, she stretched out her arm – and froze.

The earth stood still. All sound – feet scuffing on steps, chatter, the thuds and cries of the football players, wind buffeting the trees on the playing field – ceased. Nothing moved. Only one large, dark marble spun and glittered, sending flashes of pure colour – crimson, blue, gold – dappling Meena's hand like jewelled glass.

As if in slow motion, delight spread across her face and she reached further.

No. Henry lunged forwards. A thrill ran through his fingers as, shooting past Meena's, they closed on the marble, sending waves of warmth flooding up his arm. A great shout of joy gathered inside him, ready to spill into laughter. The Quintessence, it must be! It had been in the library all the time! Hidden under a floorboard at the bottom of the secret chamber, then locked away in a drawer; and old Lavvy never guessed, *he* never guessed he'd scooped it into his bag – and now it was in his possession, he could do anything he liked with it, anything in the world. Let Jake try and beat him up, he'd show him! And Ralph's blood poisoning – he could sort that out *and* never be afraid of him again. Everything would be different from now on.

But – he gripped the stone hard. There was someone else, someone at the back of his mind whose need pierced him even more deeply than any pleasure he could have in his enemies' downfall.

The shout ebbed away. Shapes and colours around him hardened. Meena stayed, arm stretched out, black plaits skimming the ground, Jake just visible behind her, one foot raised mid-step. For a split-second it was as if Henry were gazing at a photograph, or a film that had been paused. The picture shimmered.

'Meena!'

No reply. Her outline faded against the tarmac, which was tarmac no longer but – but flagstones edged with cobbles. The scattered marbles had vanished. Instead, tiny low hedges divided flower beds into triangles, the earth bare save for a few clusters of plants, stiff with frost. To his left – no grey, concrete classroom block but a long red-brick wing two storeys high, the roof sprouting turrets and spiralled chimneys. Thrusting the stone into his pocket, he swivelled round.

It was the same on his right but closer. Between him and the games field another wing stretched away, finishing, like the left-hand one, in a hexagonal tower, its domed roof black against the darkening sky. Straight ahead, where the dining hall and music block should be, a low wall ran between the towers to complete the square: a wall with a gate in the middle. From the outbuildings beyond came the thud of hooves on stable floors and a clattering on cobbles, voices giving orders, chickens clucking, the swish of water…

'No!' he swung back to the building behind, blinking hard. He was hallucinating, he must be! Yet instead of the pale wood and glass-panelled entrance to the library corridor, the wall ran unbroken to where, in its centre, framed by two stone pillars, a great oak door stood ajar giving on to a dark passage. Above and to the left candlelight grew and faded across diamond-patterned windows, as if someone, no, several people were carrying something heavy slowly up the stairs.

He closed his eyes and pressed his fists to his sides to stop the trembling. *This could not be happening.* But there was no way to block his ears to the clash of metal echoing through the doorway, nor to the sound of feet hurtling towards him from further up the passage and the cry that tore the air.

'Thomas, put your sword away, I'll not fight you!'

'No, for your cowardice you will not. Murderer!'

'I loved your father, I swear it! His death was none of my— '

'Liar! Blackheart!' The second voice rose to a screech. 'You *killed* him!'

The door lay open. Running to it Henry crossed the threshold and stared left down the passage where the voices had faded, willing his sight to adjust to the darkness.

Not quickly enough. A flash of metal, a gasp of pain, the thud of something falling heavily against wood. He could just make out two shapes, tussling together, before one wrenched a door open, thrust the other through, and slammed it shut. Then came a sound that turned Henry's stomach to lead: a key grating in an iron lock.

'Fly to your den, necromancer!' the second voice cried. 'You'll never leave – unless by sorcery!' The figure hastened to the end of the passage and disappeared.

Henry stood, staring into the darkness, unable to breathe. He must be dreaming. Either that or … The hair rose on the back of his neck. Could it be the stone's doing? He'd longed to find John and suddenly the Quintessence lay in his hand; had it granted his wish, just as it had granted John's wish for the cockerel to turn on Thomas? Transporting him back over four hundred years to Walton Hall – what, so that he could see Thomas Walton stab his foster-brother before locking him into the library to die? If so, that was awful! Yes, he'd wanted to find John; but not like this. Not to witness the last hopeless, agonising moments of his life.

His life. Plunging a hand into his pocket, Henry gripped the sphere it contained and something seemed to burst in his heart. Of course, he had the *Life Stone.* What was he waiting for? He could use it to save John! Down the passage, feeling his way along the right-hand wall until there – yes – the panelling gave way to a strip of darkness. A shallow recess, two steps leading upwards

– ah, he recognised these – to the heavy oak door. Fumbling across wood, his fingers struck something cold and metallic.

'Not so fast, Master Fowst.'

Henry let go of the key as if it had given him an electric shock.

A shadow detached itself from the wall further down the passage. A shadow dressed from head to toe in black, save for the turquoise feather nodding in its cap. As it moved, glimpses of crimson darted through the slashed velvet, matching the fiery glow of its eyes.

CHAPTER THIRTY-NINE

Save Him

Henry reeled back.

'Did – I – not – warn you' – thin lips stretched over white teeth to outline each word – '*I am not to be played with*?'

'I—' Henry's voice stuck to the back of his throat. His hands, scrabbling for a hold on the panelling behind him, slipped and slid away.

'You were to bring the Quintessence to me, not try its power yourself. How dared you awaken the flame?'

'I did – *what*?'

Darkness loomed over him, shot through with eyes that glowed red, blue, gold; colours he'd seen blazing from a black, spinning marble only moments ago. It was as though both eyes and stone were forged in the same furnace, deep within the earth.

His insides turned to water. The stone weighed against his leg, pressing through his trousers to burn his skin. His fingers curled, longing to touch it, hold it, feel its power flow through him – while at the back of his mind a voice said: *No. Forget trying to help John. The stone will control you like it controlled him, twisting your thoughts till you don't recognise them anymore. Better to hand it over quickly. Let it return to the dark place from which it came.*

'I'm s-sorry,' he whispered. 'I – I didn't mean to.' He slid his hand towards his pocket. *Quickly.* 'Here.'

'Wait. There is more you can do for me.' Mephistopheles shot out his arm.

Henry cried out. The hand hadn't touched him but it felt as if an iron manacle held his wrist, squeezing the flesh, preventing him from reaching the stone. 'Please,' he panted, 'I – I've brought you the Quintessence. That was the bargain. We're quits!'

'Not yet. You were to put it in my hands, I think.'

What? What difference did it make how he delivered the stone? *Just do it*, flashed through his mind. *Whatever the guy wants.* 'OK, I'll place it in your hands. Just – please – let me go!' He struggled to free his wrist but the invisible iron only cut deeper.

A softness entered Mephistopheles's voice. 'Go? And leave John to die?'

Henry stopped struggling. The pain in his wrist ebbed away.

'Did you not wish to save him just now?' said Mephistopheles. His words wrapped themselves around Henry's brain like fine silk. 'It lies in your power to do so.'

Save him. The voice echoed in Henry's mind another, younger one, pleading and desperate. *Find me. Help me.* What was he to do? He was here now, he couldn't just abandon John!

A velvet arm slid across his shoulder, propelling him forwards. 'You are young,' murmured Mephistopheles, 'like him. He will listen to you.'

It was like a flaw in the silk thread, briefly interrupting its smooth flow. Henry just had time to register this odd choice of words – for how could listening make any difference to John now? – before he found himself pushed through the library door.

'Save him,' hissed Mephistopheles into his ear, 'and you are free.'

Grey light filtered through the long windows at the far end of the library and fell on shapes he knew well: the book-lined walls, the two curved staircases, the gallery above. But in the bay, where Lavvy's desk should be, stood a long oak table on carved legs, holding strange metallic objects. Of course – the mathematical instruments John loved so much! And John himself – Henry's eyes flew to the recess above the right-hand stairs. Could he have made it up there?

The hand on his shoulder tightened, pressing him further into the room. At the bottom of the staircase, Mephistopheles called out softly over Henry's head, 'Master Striven.'

Henry drew in his breath. The recess lay in shadow; yet there, on the right, a strip of blackness showed the door into the secret chamber propped open by what seemed to be a pile of crumpled brown fabric leaning half against the door's edge, half on the top step to the floor below. The fabric moved and a pale face emerged, lips open as if struggling to breathe, hair clinging in dark strands to the forehead.

Dark strands that sunlight would burnish to copper.

'Master Striven,' Mephistopheles spoke again, his voice soothing as a knife dipped in honey, 'there is no need for this. What you seek is here.'

The head sank back, as if its owner were trying to draw the strength to straighten and turn towards them. His left hand clutched his side, white against the dark doublet and yet darker stain spreading across it. White, except where crimson streaked the skin.

Henry's heart beat in his throat. His muscles tensed, ready to leap up the stairs, reach the injured boy and help in any way he could – but why should Mephistopheles care? Why was he so eager for Henry to save a life that would have to be surrendered sooner or later?

He glanced at the profile beside him, the half-lidded eyes focussed on John with a strange urgency, almost a kind of hunger. The grip on his shoulder strengthened, long fingers digging between muscle and bone.

'Now, Master Fowst, your opportunity.' Mephistopheles licked his lips. 'Hold out the Quintessence.'

Henry clenched his fist against his side. *Don't do it,* he told himself, *don't take the thing into your hand. Who knows what will follow?* But his hand slid to his pocket, he couldn't help it, searching for that smooth, round shape whose touch – ah, there! – sent a delicious shiver up his arm. Drawing it out, he let his shoulders relax, exulting in the energy that coursed through his body. Oh, this felt good, this surge of life, of power! Why shouldn't he use it to help John, at least from his present suffering? To heal that cruel, gaping wound – how could that be bad? Mounting the stairs two at a time, he held his hand straight out before him, uncurling the fingers.

A tongue of blue flame leaped into the gloom, sending a ray across the figure lying propped against the chamber opening. A tremor crossed John's face; his listless gaze cleared and flew to Henry's, cracked lips opening in a cry of joy. His right hand, resting beside him, stretched forward.

Henry froze. Crimson stained John's forefinger and ran in rivulets down his palm. Behind him on the chamber floor, a single word lay scrawled in thick, uneven strokes on a fragment of paper.

Low, almost tender, Mephistopheles's voice reached up to him. 'Speak, Master Fowst. Bid him take back the Life Stone. Then he will have no need of – *mercy*.'

That word. It zipped through Henry like an electric shock. His arm wavered. Yet why? Mephistopheles was right! In his palm lay all power, all healing, all safety…

There is no safety.

Henry staggered. Blue and gold light danced across the gallery. John had said nothing. Yet the voice was his, he knew it! Speaking with the same urgency that haunted his dreams, begging Henry to put back the message he was writing now, here, in his own life blood…

Not the message. It hit him like a thunderbolt. That wasn't what he had to put back.

From the floor below came an exclamation of impatience: 'Give it to him! Why do you delay? Are four hundred years'– the voice rose, almost to shrillness – 'not enough for you?'

Henry clenched his jaw. *No safety*, he repeated in his mind, forcing his thoughts back on themselves, pushing against the sense of power sweeping up his arm and through his body. *Let the stone take over and you are lost.* He tightened his hand to block the flames now shooting from the Quintessence, the edges of his fingers glowing crimson, and gritted his teeth as a burning sensation spread through his skin. 'John,' he said, 'here is the Quintessence. Do I give it to you, to use its power whichever way you want; or do I – *put it back*?'

John's eyes flickered. Closing, they seemed to sink further into their sockets, pale lashes resting on bone. His fingers, almost touching Henry's, faltered.

A gasp from below. 'Take it, John Striven, take it and live! How else can you keep your promise to your master? Do you think *Thomas* will preserve his books if you are not there to protect them?'

John's mouth tautened and his head jolted backwards, as if he'd been struck. He opened his eyes to gaze at Henry but his arm, weakening, fell by his side, sending the scrap of paper floating deeper into the chamber beside him.

And in a flash, Henry understood. *Evil charms call forth*

evil demons… nor, if the bargain once be struck, can the soul be saved except by God's mercy.

The soul. John's soul. That was what this was all about.

'Give it to him!' Mephistopheles's words lashed out like a whip.

'Shall I, John?' Henry felt as if he were gripping hot lead. Blinking hard, he forced his tone to hold steady. 'Your life – or your soul. The choice is yours.'

A soft movement of eyelashes, the slightest shake of John's head. His lips parted; he was trying to speak! Bending forwards, Henry knelt to catch the words, faint but unmistakeable.

'Put – it – back.' John's breath came out in a sigh. The effort seemed to have taken his last scrap of strength and his head lolled against the chamber door behind him.

'*Fool!*' Mephistopheles's voice rose to a screech. 'Traitor to your master's dying wish!'

'No!' Grasping the book case with his left hand, Henry hauled himself to his feet. 'John,' he panted, 'your promise is safe. It isn't your life that will preserve your master's books. It's – this!'

Setting his teeth against the aching in his shoulder, he raised his arm and hurled the stone over John's head and into the secret chamber. Flames exploded in the darkness and vanished like firework sparks. From deep within the chamber came a crash as the stone hit the wall and bounced down steps to the floor below.

Let it lie where it fell. Hidden it cannot harm.

Henry staggered at the sudden release of immense

weight. Nursing his right arm, sore but – oh the relief – loose and free, he watched as a wave of calm flowed over John's features, smoothing his brow and cheek. The hand holding his side relaxed, his right shoulder sank and he toppled backwards. Too late Henry lunged to catch him: hitting the top step, John rolled sideways and fell with a thud to the floor below.

From behind came a shriek of rage. 'Villain! Wretch! You will pay – your precious friend Ralph will pay. The bargain is forfeit!'

'No!' Henry wheeled round. 'I kept my side of it! I brought you the Quintessence and you refused to take it until you'd finished with me. That wasn't fair.'

Mephistopheles's eyes blazed. 'Miserable piece of scum,' he spat, 'who are you to tell *me*?'

Henry gripped the chamber door with both hands to stop them from shaking. 'But I was fair to you!' he cried. 'Even when you demanded another bargain. "Save John and you're free," you said. Well' – he paused to take breath – 'I did save him. *From you!*'

Mephistopheles flinched, as if struck. '*Lying – deceiving – traitorous – vermin!*' he shrieked, his smooth features contorted out of all recognition. 'You dare play at words and meanings with – with *me*!' Choking, he hurled himself at the gallery.

Henry shrank back. Two arms strained to reach him through the railings, fingers curved like – like claws. A shimmer, like wind over corn, ran over Mephistopheles's velvet-clad figure, from the splash of turquoise in his cap down to his fine leather boots, transforming all to a black, shaggy, four-legged creature, its mouth wide open in a gleaming snarl.

Henry cried out. In the same moment came a tremendous crack from below, as of floorboards ripped open, and a wind, hot and fiery, rushed up at him, like the blast from a furnace. A howl of frustration rent the air as, for a split second, the huge black dog stood outlined against a wall of flame; then the flames swallowed it up, drawing it down through the library floor.

Henry's legs gave way and he fell sideways, his body crumpled on the chamber threshold.

★

'He's coming round.'

'Thank heaven for that. I'll fetch Mr Robertson.'

A creak of skirts followed by stilettos clicking down wooden stairs; sounds more welcome to Henry than any other in the world.

'No laughing matter, y'know. You gave us a helluva scare, fainting like that.' A freckle-smudged face looked down on him before turning to the black square cut into the book case. 'And what the heck is this?'

'Charlie,' Henry croaked. 'It's good to see you.' Waves of shaking coursed through him and something bubbled up inside, laughter or tears he couldn't be sure but whatever it was, no way could he hold on to it.

Charlie's eyebrows drew together. 'You too,' he

mumbled. 'When Meena came running in, yelling you'd vanished, all I could think was that you were back in here, rifling through all your precious books. Seems I was right.'

From behind Henry's head came the sound of a door closing again and a rustle of skirts. 'He's not in his office,' sighed Mrs D'Arcy. 'Charles, you go for help, I'll stay.'

'No.' Henry grabbed Charlie's arm and heaved himself up. 'I'm fine. I'll be OK. I've just got to see' – leaning on the gallery rail he stared downwards. The polished boards of the library floor stretched smoothly from wall to wall. Not a crack – or sign of charring – in sight. He let out a long breath.

'Don't know why you're looking down there,' said Charlie. 'Up here's where the excitement is. Look!'

Crouching at the chamber opening, Henry stretched his eyes wide but it was no good.

'Here.' Charlie thrust a slim rectangular shape in his hand. 'My phone. It's got a torch.'

The narrow white beam danced over the floorboards, picking out the steps down, and just to the left of them, the sheer drop into blackness below. Leaning over, Henry lowered his arm.

The skin prickled on the back of his neck. Beside him he heard Charlie's sharp intake of breath. The point of light travelled over a lattice of bone and shreds of brown material, a glint of metal and, then, unmistakeably, the shape of a skull turned upwards, dark sockets gazing straight into his soul.

CHAPTER FORTY

Resolutions

'Henry! Henree! It's you, look!'

'Well, I will, if you get out of the way.'

Henry peeled his sister's hand off the *Daily Herald*. "Friday, 2nd February" stayed printed in mirror-writing on her skin and some of the ink on the newspaper was smudged but not enough to damage the photograph on the front page. A large black square took up much of the picture, flanked on one side by indistinct shapes of books, and on the other by himself in an awkward crouching position, which accounted for the fixed grin on his face.

Grimacing, he read the headline and article below.

"HISTORIC MURDER VICTIM DISCOVERED AT LOCAL SCHOOL

Police were called to Northwell School on Wednesday afternoon to investigate a crime committed over four hundred years ago. Student Henry Fowst stumbled across a skeleton hidden in a secret chamber in the school library.

'I was researching for my homework,' said Henry, 13, 'and the book case suddenly opened. I nearly jumped out of my skin.'"

Homework? Well, near enough.

"On searching the chamber, Headmaster Alistair Robertson, 48, confirmed the find. 'It's very exciting for the school,' he said. 'We knew from the existence of the Walton Book Collection that Northwell School was a special place. This discovery adds a whole new chapter to its history.'

The skeleton has been removed for examination but it is thought that tests will reveal it to belong to John Striven, who lived in a house on the school site in the late sixteenth century. Documentary evidence in the City Library strongly suggests that he was unlawfully killed by his foster-brother, Thomas Walton."

Yup, he'd made sure of that. All the information the headmaster needed lay in the Reverend Timothy Liddell's letter in the City Library. By directing him there, Henry could keep John Striven's diary out of the picture altogether. With luck that would stay where it was, concealed in the shelf with all the faded, battered books… Why not? No one knew it existed. John's secret could stay undiscovered, as it had been for over four hundred years.

The same for the Quintessence. All the excitement

focussed on the skeleton. No one would bother to look for a strange round stone wedged under a floorboard near the bottom of the stairs. There it could lie, as it had done for hundreds of years, silently protecting library and hall from damage, fire, rebuilding even, preserving forever Northwell School's Elizabethan heart.

From the passage came the sound of a key in a lock. Rachel slid off the chair and ran to the door. 'Mum, come quick, Henry's in the newspaper!'

'Really?' His mum appeared, still in her coat, her face red from the early morning cold. 'That's wonderful! I still can't believe it was you who discovered it all.'

'What's so wonderful?' Dad entered, a mug of tea in his hand. 'Shouldn't you kids be getting off to school? Ah.' His gaze travelled from the newspaper on the table to Henry's face. 'So, your fame's spread, eh. Well done, son.'

Henry couldn't believe it. His dad's eyes – did they actually twinkle? Somehow his own face wouldn't keep straight. 'Yeah, Dad,' he grinned. 'Wait, I'll read it.'

'No.' Crossing the room, Dad whisked the paper out of his hand. 'If my son's clever enough to make the front page, *I* want to read about it myself.'

Henry's hands stayed hanging in the air. '*You?*'

'Well – not immediately.' Dad shifted his weight slightly and glanced away. But almost at once his eyes were back on Henry's and his voice held a note Henry had never heard before. 'You got me thinking, son. What you said about – about not trying. So I phoned that number. Actually,' he coughed, 'I went to see them. And – and you were right. They were nice about it. Said I wasn't alone and they could help me.' He closed his eyes. 'I can't tell you how good that felt.'

'*Dad*!' Henry's breath came out in a rush as he launched himself in the air. The strong, warm arms wrapped round him and the hairs on his father's chest tickled his nose through the clean, sweet-smelling shirt and he couldn't speak.

'Group hug!' cried a voice from somewhere just above his waist. He turned to draw in Rachel, as his mother's arm – still in the scratchy coat sleeve – went round his back.

'Enough.' His dad pulled away. 'Come on now. School.' He stood back, blinking. 'Shoes, anorak – quick, Rachel. Then we can walk your brother to the bus stop.'

'What'll they do with him?' Rachel scrabbled round for her trainers. 'With John – thingummy. I mean, will they bury him?'

'Striven,' said Henry. 'Yes. In the churchyard, I hope. But first there'll be a' – he paused to recall exactly what the head had said –'an inquest. To find out how he died.'

'Huh,' she snorted. 'You told them that already.'

'They still have to do tests and things to make sure the body – skeleton – really is that old so they can match it with – with what happened.' His voice trailed away as John's face filled his mind, not as he last saw it but how he must have looked when touching those scientific

262

instruments, or playing with his sisters at home; the green eyes wide under hair redder even than his, mouth curved in a smile above the soft chin. How could he think of him as a skeleton, a bundle of crumbling bones lying in the bottom of a hidden chamber?

'Come *on*, Rachel.' Dad appeared from the passage, holding her anorak.

Behind him, Mum's voice floated round the door. 'Oh, and more good news. That poor school friend of yours, the one with blood poisoning' – coatless, she came back into the room – 'he should be going home soon. Sally Brown in Critical Care told me. He turned the corner on – Wednesday, I think it was. Very suddenly, apparently.'

Henry nodded. Yes, it would've been Wednesday. At about ten to two. The moment he fulfilled his side of the bargain and beat Mephistopheles, once and for all.

CHAPTER FORTY-ONE

Quits at Last

Emerging from the tunnel into the playground, Henry scanned the clusters of people and found what he was looking for.

Between him and the classroom, a tall, fair-haired figure stood near the wall of the dining room block, surrounded by an awe-struck group. His left arm, bandaged from shoulder to wrist, lay in a sling. Right hand thrust into his pocket, he leaned back slightly on one foot – an attempt at a casual, easy look, somewhat belied by the pallor of his face – as he spoke to his audience.

Henry drew near to listen.

'So this bloody great Rottweiler hurls itself at me out of nowhere, halfway down Walton Road. Don't know how no one else saw it but yeah, I suppose I was a bit late for school. I fought it off, of course, but not before it gave me this' – he lifted his arm in its sling. 'Oh, and blood poisoning.'

'And the police haven't even found the owner!' exploded Jake. 'Or the dog. It's unbelievable!'

Not really, thought Henry. *Nothing like as unbelievable as if they do.* 'Hi, Ralph,' he said. 'You feeling better?'

Ralph gazed at him for a moment before replying. 'Yeah. Thanks.'

The knots of people in the playground began to break up. It was nearly time for register.

Charlie came over to Henry. 'Meena's looking for you,' he said. 'Apparently you promised to teach her marbles last week just before you bolted?'

Ah. Yes. That had taken some explaining. Especially the bit about the stunning marble that turned out to be just, um, a really beautiful galaxy. Which Henry – sadly – no longer owned. 'Yeah. Lunch time today,' he said. 'I'll make it up to her.'

Ralph shifted his gaze from Henry's face to his school bag, slung over his shoulder. 'Got a moment?' he said. 'There's something I want to ask you.'

Incredible, Henry thought. The guy was still after his Northwell essay. Taking a deep breath, he said, 'Sure.' *OK, bring it on. I'm ready for you.*

'Right, you guys,' Ralph nodded at the others, 'I'll see you indoors.'

Jake frowned. 'You want to watch him,' he muttered. 'One minute he's in the playground chucking marbles around, the next he's disappeared and knocking holes in the library. OK, OK, I'm going.'

Charlie looked at Henry, eyebrows raised.

'It's fine,' said Henry. 'You go in. See you in a sec.'

Charlie gave him such a big grin it was all Henry

could do not to laugh. *Oh Charlie, if only you knew*, he thought. But it was better this way.

'Good to have you back, mate.' Charlie clapped Ralph on the (uninjured) shoulder. 'Just get that arm better, all right? We play St Olaf's after half-term and I don't want to even think about our chances if you're not there.'

'Will do.' With a smile Ralph watched Charlie join the others making for the classroom block. Once the door swung to behind them, he closed his eyes and let his head fall back against the wall. Tiredness seemed to wash over him, leaving his face pale and drawn.

'I wasn't supposed to come in today,' he said, after a moment. 'But I wanted to. Know why? 'Cos of the essay deadline, of course. In the bag, is it?'

Henry tightened his hand around the strap. 'Yes.'

Ralph nodded. 'With your name on it?'

Henry drew himself up. 'Yes.'

'Good. Right, well, better hand it in, hadn't you? Not going to do much good left there.'

Henry nearly let the bag fall from his shoulder. 'You mean you're not going to make me – and you won't –?'

'Look, Henry.' Ralph raised his left arm in its sling a little way from his body. 'Even if I wanted that laptop – and somehow it's just not important anymore – no one's going to believe I could've written an essay while nearly dying from blood poisoning. Besides' – he looked away – 'my mum says you came to see me in hospital. That was – nice of you. No one else did.'

Henry stared down at the ground. 'You looked pretty bad,' he said.

'So I hear. Even gave my dad a shock. I couldn't believe it when I woke up and there he was, and he looked so tired and so old but – but as if the best thing in the world had just happened.' Closing his mouth tight, Ralph gazed across the playground. A muscle in his cheek twitched. 'I've been pretty mean to you. Sorry.'

A strange warmth rushed through Henry; not something he'd ever expected to feel towards Ralph. 'It's fine. It's all over,' he said. 'I'm just glad you're OK.' *You'll never know how glad*, he thought. *At least, I hope you won't.*

Ralph nodded. 'Me too. So, Hamf- I mean,' he corrected himself with a grin, 'Henry – what do you reckon? Quits?'

'Yeah.' Henry grinned back. 'Quits. Thanks, Ralph.'

'No problem. Guess we'd better go in now.'

Go in, now? When all Henry wanted to do was run around the playground, throwing his school bag in the air? His problems were over! He need never be scared of Ralph again.

But Ralph was right. Now wasn't the time. Quelling the fizzing inside his chest, Henry fell into step beside his new friend. 'Amazing,' he said. 'Here you are, back at school again, when less than a week ago you were nearly a goner.'

'Yup,' Ralph nodded.

267

'And all because of a poodle! Who'd believe it?'

'How the hell did you…?' Ralph stopped himself. 'No, a Rottweiler.'

'A Rottweiler, of course.' Henry hit himself on the forehead. 'Did I say poodle? I meant Rottweiler.' Reaching the door to the classroom block, he pulled it open. 'Coming?'

A few paces away Ralph stared at him, a puzzled expression on his face. Opening his mouth to say something, he seemed to change his mind and instead walked slowly towards the door. By the time he took hold of the handle, puzzlement had grown into thoughtfulness and he followed Henry silently upstairs.

Mastering a grin, Henry led the way to the classroom.

Epilogue

Henry opened the gate. Patches of sunshine dappled the ivy leaves and warmed pools of grasses growing between the mottled stones. In the shadow of the yew tree, clusters of bluebells glimmered: deep mauve, white, pink. In the oak tree a blackbird sang.

Fresh earth had been turned over the grave. He laid his school bag down carefully beside it. The laptop – a shining, top of the range Adoney model – had a case to protect it, but even so.

Straightening up, he focussed on the bright new cuts in the stone, the lines of the letters continuing the sentence that had never been finished.

"…And of
JOHN, his son, who died on
16ᵗʰ December, 1586, aged 13 years.
'For this my son was dead, and is alive again;
he was lost, and is found.'
Luke 15: 24"

Henry felt a prickling behind his eyes. 'Goodbye, John,' he whispered. 'Your soul's safe now. He can't get it back.'

Blinking, he hoisted his bag on to his shoulder and set off for home.